COLLATERAL DAMAGE

Stories
Second Edition

KEVIN C. JONES

MILSPEAK BOOKS

An imprint of MilSpeak Foundation, Inc.

Grateful thanks to Press 53 for publishing the first edition of this collection, and to the editors of the following publications for first publishing these stories:

Atticus Review, "The Distance from There to Here"

Boomtown: Explosive Writing from Ten Years of the Queens University of Charlotte MFA Program (anthology), "Collateral Damage"

Cobalt Review, "Safety"

Monkeybicycle, "She Was Only a Bagel Seller's Daughter"

O-Dark-Thirty: The Literary Journal of the Veterans Writing Project, "First Person Shooter"

Prime Number Magazine, "Education"

r.kv.r.y., "The Edge of Water" and "Pugilist"

Manufactured in the United States of America

Library of Congress Cataloging-in-Publication Data

Jones, Kevin

Library of Congress Control Number: 2021947307
ISBN 978-1-7378676-3-0 (paperback)
ISBN 978-1-7378676-7-8 (epub)

Editing by: M.C. Armstrong
Cover art by: www.BoldBookCovers.com
Formatting by: www.BoldBookCovers.com

MilSpeak Foundation, Inc.
5097 York Martin Road
Liberty, NC 27298
www.MilSpeakFoundation.org

For My Girls

PREFACE

If you had asked my friends from high school, many of whom I'm still fortunate enough to be close to today—now three decades later—they would have said I was the last person in the world to join the military, let alone the Marine Corps.

The fact I did join, and chose to serve in the infantry, is something even I still find surprising to this day. I've never looked like what most people envision when they think of a Marine. I wasn't an athlete. I didn't have a burning need to serve my country against all enemies, foreign and domestic. What I did have was a desire to do something adventurous while I still could before I succumbed to the (to my young mind) inevitable life of suburban living, marriage, kids, and some sort of boring office job for the rest of my life. Things I was privileged enough to take for granted at the time and viewed as a sort of middle-class purgatory that I wanted to put off as long as possible. Clearly, I knew nothing, but that's what the Marine Corps depends on.

I wanted to prove to myself that I could do something challenging. An experience I would remember for the rest of my life. The Corps was happy to give me that opportunity.

During my training at Camp Pendleton I often escaped to Los Angeles on the weekends. A native Californian, I had friends who attended college there and I would tag along as they went to parties in Hollywood, Pasadena, and Venice Beach. In a world of long hair and rock and roll I was a curiosity with my shaved head and Marine Corps mandated conservative attire. Back on the base I felt similarly disconnected. I learned to enjoy the routine, the discipline, the camaraderie, but so much of it felt performative to me, like wearing a costume. For a long time, I thought I might have made a mistake in joining. That I just didn't fit. It wasn't until much later that I realized just how many other servicemembers felt exactly as I did. How many others would spend the rest of their lives trying to write their experiences, both in and out of uniform, fiction and truth, in an attempt to make some kind of sense of it all.

The first edition of this collection, published by Press 53, was my effort to do exactly this. I was exploring the effect military service has on a variety of characters. Some who served. Others who were veterans, family members, service-adjacent, and the like. I wrote these over the better part of a decade, the oldest when I was an undergraduate in California after leaving the Marine Corps, then as a graduate student in Charlotte, North Carolina, then others while I taught English at a university in Tampa. It wasn't until I was putting them together for this collection that I realized all the characters had a military connection. This wasn't a conscious choice, but probably an inevitable one; although I'm many years away from active service, the Marine Corps is always there, whether I want it to be or not.

While preparing this second edition, the President announced a full and final withdrawal of all American military forces from Afghanistan, effectively ending the country's longest war with the stroke of a pen. Politicians and historians will argue whether any of it was worth the cost in blood and treasure—if the loss of thousands of overwhelmingly young lives changed anything. Those who served will have their own answers, even if most will never say them out loud. Veterans know wars never actually end. They remain carried inside by those who fought them, taken out to look at from time to time. To hold. To remember. Sometimes on purpose, more often accidently, when something unexpectedly jars the memory. With the smell of gunpowder, metal lubricants, humidity and rotting vegetation, time compresses, and the veteran is once again young. Uniformed. Back on deployment in a faraway land. Sense memory as time travel, revealing that events, long thought forgotten, will always have a hold.

I am grateful to have had the chance to help others write their stories, to show their truth to the world. I am grateful to be able to share my truth through this second edition of my collection, even if it is through fiction. All fiction, of course, contains a bit of truth. Sometimes more than a bit. Some of the stories in this collection are almost completely true. Others barely at all. The truth, like my service, I carry inside, just for me, waiting for it to emerge when I least expect it.

CONTENTS

The Edge of Water

That November after Iraq, after all the surgeries on my leg, after I could get around with crutches instead of a wheelchair, after the bruising was only a memory and the concussion toned down to a few minor headaches that only bothered me in bright sunlight or movie theatres, I found myself in California again. I was having a beer with my best friend, Greg, and his new wife, Chelsea. Greg was the creative director of a PR firm. He'd told me the name once, but I couldn't remember. He seemed to jump companies every other week and all of their names sounded the same to me. The bar was his idea. He said that I needed to get out more and that he wasn't going to allow me to spend my entire convalescent leave in my hotel bedroom with the shades drawn. He was talking about his new hobby, real estate.

"You should look into getting something, Kyle," he said. "The market is totally stacked for buyers right now."

"Right, stacked."

I stared down at his wedding ring. It looked like he'd won the Super Bowl.

"I know you don't have a lot of cash," he said. "But I can put you in contact with some people. Pull a few strings, get you a good deal."

"I'm still stationed in Hawaii, why would I want something here?"

"Investment. Besides, you aren't going to be there that much longer, right?"

"I don't know," I said, sipping on my drink. Greg loved dark beer so we'd met at a British pub downtown. They didn't have anything Mexican so when the bartender asked what I wanted I told him "Anything that isn't the color of mud." What I got was something that looked and tasted like overpriced Budweiser.

Greg kept trying not to look at my leg, at the brace I'm only allowed to take off in the shower. He was trying to be casual about it, but when you're deliberately trying to not look at something it's just that much more obvious. Chelsea wasn't much better. With her slick, page boy haircut and designer clothes she looked like someone out of a silent movie: Dorothy Parker in Prada. She kept staring at me and I wondered if she was going to say something. I wore a beanie to keep my head warm but you could still see the shrapnel scars on my neck. When I'd had enough I deliberately looked directly into her eyes, smiling as she quickly dropped her gaze down to my arms resting on the table between us.

"That's an interesting tattoo," she said, looking at the inside of my left forearm. Exposed from where I'd pushed up the sleeves of my thermal shirt was the black silhouette of a winged skull with crossed tridents behind it, the words *Aut Vincere, Aut Mori* in Latin below, USMC in Old English script above.

Victory or Death.

Greg looked out of the window, watched rain spatter against panes, run into gutters.

"He's got a bunch," he said.

"Really?"

Chelsea looked at me with new interest.

Diamonds hung in her ears like stars.

"One or two," I said.

"One or two?" Greg laughed. "Christ, what have you got, really, fifteen or sixteen now?"

"One less than I used to. The surgeons took care of the one on my leg."

Chelsea looked down at her Amaretto Sour, back up at me. She had brown eyes with long, thick lashes that made me think of someone else.

My team was coming back from patrol. There were five of us in the Humvee: Ortiz was driving, Alexander, Weatherford, and Simone were in the back seat. I rode shotgun. It was surreal, the drive. We had just spent three days in the ass-end of the city looking for insurgents. Sixteen-hour patrols, trying to scrounge up any source of intel we could find, any sign of where the bad guys might be. Kicking in doors when people wouldn't open them for us, staring into the faces of children and old men. People we terrified with our helmets and goggles and rifles. Now, here we were, after all that, stuck in traffic.

"Just like L.A., right Sergeant?" Ortiz said. "Just like home."

"If this is what L.A. is like, it's no wonder y'all can't fucking drive," Weatherford said, reaching over the seat with his huge, dark hands and smacking Ortiz on the helmet.

I turned around and looked at him.

"I've been to D.C., Weatherford," I said. "It's no fucking picnic either."

"Too true, too true," he said. "But I'll sure as shit take the Beltway over this bullshit here any day of the fucking week."

He reached into his IBA and pulled out a cigarette.

"Let me get one of those," I said.

He looked at me.

"Thought you didn't smoke."

"I don't. Mission's over, we're in one piece, I feel like relaxing a bit. That okay with you, Lance Corporal?" I was fucking with him by pulling rank. When there weren't any officers around I never made anyone call me sergeant. They were my friends, my team. Ortiz was the only one who addressed people by their rank, a habit he hadn't broken yet, born of his time in Boot Camp and the School of Infantry the year before. More than once I'd told him if he didn't relax I'd shoot him myself.

Weatherford handed me a smoke, then his lighter. "It's your lungs, man," he said. "But I will collect later."

"Deal."

Alexander said, "Don't talk about being in one piece. You'll jinx us."

Weatherford snorted a laugh. "Fuck that superstitious bullshit."

"Whatever, dog." Ortiz looked over the steering wheel at the crowds and traffic all around us. "It's bad luck to talk about how good things are when we're not back at the FOB yet. It's. . . what do they call it? Tempting fate."

I took a deep drag off of my cigarette, coughed once, exhaled.

"See," Weatherford said. "I knew you didn't smoke. That's a waste of a good cigarette right there."

"Fuck you," I said. "I'll buy you more when we get back."

"Damn straight."

We drove another few blocks and traffic slowed to a crawl. There was some kind of accident up ahead of us. People shouting, waving their arms. Some guy in a polo shirt and shitty slacks had a cell phone up to his ear. I finished half of my smoke, rolled down the window, and tossed it out into the street. We stopped at the edge of the intersection and that's when I saw the woman.

"Head's up," I said.

"She walked out of a nearby building and made her way towards us. Everyone in the Humvee turned to watch. She looked left and right, nervous, taking small, hesitant steps across the pavement.

"Sergeant..." Simone's voice from directly behind me. I could hear him adjusting in his seat to bring his weapon around and point it at the woman.

"Wait," I said. "Just a second. She's alone. Something's up."

I'd never seen a woman travel without a male escort in Iraq the entire time I'd been there. I had my own rifle turned outboard, the barrel pointing out of the window as she approached me. Plastic bags blew across the street like tumbleweeds. I kept the muzzle aimed at her chest.

Her body was hidden behind the black folds of her burka and all I could see were her eyes, dark brown against the pale mocha skin of her face. They were beautiful, with long, dark lashes and an intensity, an energy I'd never seen before or since.

"This is insane," Alexander said. "She must need some kind of serious help or something if she's coming to talk to us in public like this."

"She must need food," I said. "Or water. She must have kids."

"Sergeant?" Ortiz motioned at the road ahead of us. The traffic had cleared. It was okay to go now. "We can tell Civil Affairs or whoever when we get back to the FOB. This is their kind of shit, not ours."

The woman continued towards us, walking into the street now.

"Just a sec, Ortiz," I said, reaching down to get a bottle of water and some rations from my pack. "COIN. Hearts and minds, remember? Let me give her something and we'll go."

Then she detonated.

"Well," Chelsea said. "You look pretty good, considering."

"Considering what?" I said.

"You know." She nodded towards my crutches, the brace on my right leg. I could sense her discomfort, wondered what she'd tell Greg in their car on the ride home. "Greg told me it was bad. You were lucky, I guess."

Lucky. Sure. My leg was covered with long, erratic scars still prominent despite hours of skin grafts. The docs at the combat hospital told me that it was always going to look this way. But I am lucky. Lucky that I was ducking down behind the door of the Humvee when the blast went off. Lucky I only got "light shrapnel" over the entire right side of my body. Lucky I wasn't looking directly at the explosion, like Ortiz, who lost his eyes, or Simone, who'd taken his helmet off right before we stopped and was killed instantly.

"Yeah, I'm lucky," I said, too loud in a room full of otherwise civil civilian conversation. A room full of people who'd probably never faced anything more dangerous than ordering a cup of coffee in the morning.

Chelsea looked down at the floor and I immediately felt like shit. Greg leaned across the table towards me.

"Dude," he said in a low whisper. "Relax. People are staring." I looked around and noticed that he was right. I was playing the part of Angry Veteran right out of central casting. I took a large drink of my beer and felt my fists unclench, my heart beating in my temples. Chelsea looked at me, said something, but I couldn't make it out. For a moment, everything became muffled, like I was underwater, and I wondered if it was the swelling in my brain coming back. The doctors told me to stay away from alcohol, but that was over a month ago, and I was only on my first beer. "What?" I said to Chelsea in what I hoped was a quieter voice. Around the room people drank and laughed and shimmered in my vision. After a moment sounds became clear again.

"I said, I'm sorry."

I finished my beer, stared at the empty glass, wondered if I should order another. Greg beat me to it. "Two more," he said, flagging down a waitress as she walked by.

"It's okay," I said to Chelsea. "It's just…" I let the words hang in the air like smoke.

"What?" Greg leaned in close, almost whispering. "It's just what?"

"I ordered them to stop," I said. "Ortiz, my driver, he hadn't even been in the Corps for a fucking year yet." I looked around the room, noticed a woman with long, straight hair the color of snow sitting at the bar across from our table. I watched as she drank a glass of white wine, waiting, hoping for her to make eye contact with me, but she never did. It doesn't matter; I wouldn't have known what to say to her. I remembered the blast, the way Ortiz's eye sockets looked like they were packed with jelly, the sounds of screams that took me a long time to realize were my own. "Simone's wife had a baby while we were over there. A girl." I looked at Greg. "He never got to hold her, to meet her. All because I ordered them to stop."

"You didn't know."

"I should have," I said. "It's not like it was the first time I'd been there."

Back in my room at the Naval Hospital in Hawaii, a Purple Heart still sat in its box, unopened, on my nightstand. "You need to think about the future," Greg said. "About what you're going to do next when all of this is over with."

"I can't think that far ahead."

"Start." He took another sip of his beer. "You talk to your dad lately?"

"He sends me an email every now and again," I said. "You know my dad; he blames the president for what happened to me."

"He may have a point," Chelsea said.

I looked at Greg. "You know we've never been that close."

"Yeah, well, I read somewhere that traumatic injury can change that."

He laughed. "Didn't you used to go to the beach together?"

"Yeah, when I was a little kid. Jesus, I'd forgotten about that. When my parents were still married, we used to rent a cabin near Bodega Bay at the end of summer each year. What made you think of that?"

The last Labor Day weekend we spent together as a family before everything imploded my father rented a cabin on the beach for us. It was so cold there, and I wondered how that was possible when it was still summer. On the last day he took me down past the sand dunes and we walked along the shore, my feet numb and pink in the icy water. We went into the surf together and I held onto his leg as the waves crashed into us. I was small, just a kid, and I was afraid that the current would carry me out to sea. I don't think my dad realized that, just by being there, he was saving my life. That just by letting me hold onto him, at the edge of the water, he was keeping me from washing away with the tide. It's the last good memory I have of my father, and I can't even see his face in it. Just the waves washing over us, my arms wrapped around his leg, and the sea stretching on forever to the end of the world.

"We just spent a weekend up there about a month ago," Greg said. "I remembered you used to talk about it."

"It's been years."

"Call him. Let him know how you're doing." He dropped a bone-colored business card onto the table in front of me. "And call this guy. I'm telling you, he'll hook you up with a good deal on a house."

"I'll think about it."

"Hey." Greg leaned across the table and squeezed my arm. "There are other things you can do with your life, that's all I'm trying to say."

Even with all of the physical therapy I'd been doing, the doctors told me it could be months, maybe years, before I ever ran again, but that my military career was probably over. I'd never really thought about reenlisting but hearing that I couldn't made me realize that I wasn't sure what I was going to do.

It didn't feel right, me sitting there, enjoying a cold beer in a bar while people I knew were still overseas. Still patrolling at night, kicking in doors, looking for bad guys. Today, four civilian contractors were found on the side of the road next to their burned SUV, shot in the head, execution style, left to bloat and rot in the afternoon sun. Last week a truck full of Mississippi National Guardsmen were killed when their convoy drove past a car rigged with explosives. The week before that, an Air Force jet got the wrong coordinates and dropped a bomb on someone's apartment, killing an entire family. They sent a Civil Affairs team to apologize on behalf of the United States, but there wasn't anyone left to talk to.

We stay for a few more beers and then Greg takes me back to my hotel. The next day I fly to Hawaii where the Naval Hospital releases me back to my unit. To the Rear Detachment. Everyone else is still over there. Still fighting.

During the next few months in Hawaii, where the entire world was a shock of green and blue and high, wet heat that made my uniform stick to my skin, Command makes me see the chaplain once a week. I nodded a lot. I told him I was fine. I said that I looked forward to my leg fully healing so that I could get on with my life. I said that, even though the doctors finally figured out that my leg would fully heal, I knew my time in the Marine Corps was coming to an end.

"So, what are you not telling me, son?" The chaplain said. "What are you still afraid of ?"

"Nothing," I said. "It already happened."

"You ever talk to anyone else about this? About what happened?"

"No, sir," I said. "I'm okay, really. I'm fine."

Today, at the barracks, in my room, there are a dozen emails on my computer. All of them from my father. All of them unopened. There are letters from Simone's wife. Pictures of his daughter. A description of the funeral I couldn't attend because I was still in the hospital. This morning, someone in Admin told me that Ortiz is doing better. He's living with his mother in Baldwin Park, trying to learn Braille so that he can go to college. He turned twenty last month.

I open one of the emails from my father and it's a photo of me and him when I was a kid. We're standing on the beach. I'm all elbows and knees with a red pail and shovel in my hand, my father next to me with his arm around my shoulder.

I pick up the phone. I try to dial but I can't. My hands are shaking.

Education

Psychology

G wen?" Tom is looking at me over his sub sandwich from the deli counter in the cafeteria.

"What?"

"What if you could kill someone and get away with it?"

I don't know how he eats those things, with mayonnaise squirting out of the side like snot and all of that cheap processed turkey and pickles and shit he puts on it. I ignore him and go back to my Diet Coke but he's insistent today and it looks like I might just have to pay attention this time.

"So what?" I say. "What if you could?"

"Who would you kill?"

You'd think it'd be a long list, wouldn't you? I mean, anyone in the world and nothing would happen to you. No one would know. Just snap your fingers and someone's gone. It's not. A long list, I mean. There actually aren't that many people I'd kill. That I know, anyway. I'm leaving out third-world dictators and human rights violators and most of the football team and the guy who invented algebra. Of course, he's probably dead already, right? I mean, algebra's been around for a while now, so why waste space on the list for him? Like I said, it's a short list, and no, my mother and father aren't on it, although you might think they would be. If you knew me, I mean.

And you don't.

"I don't know," I say. "I'd have to think about it."

"Oh," he says. He looks disappointed. I think he has a big list. I think he wants to tell someone. I think he's afraid that if he seems too enthusiastic someone will report him to the principal or a teacher or something and that'll be it. Schools nowadays, they have a low tolerance for that sort of thing. Talking about death, I mean. Killing, lists of fantasy homicides and all that. I'm sure you understand.

They say that the metal detectors at the front doors are to protect us, but we know better. It's for them: teachers, parents, staff.

I'm not stupid. I watch the news. I know all about the shootings and bombings at those schools in the Midwest. I've had my mandatory sensitivity training just like everyone else here. I watch what I say.

I learned to watch what I say after my fight in gym class last semester. After my meetings with the police and the school psychiatrist and the MMMPI. After lots of ink blots and no car for a month. After that the school believed me when I said I was sorry for punching out that girl in the locker room when she called me a dyke. I'm pretty sure they believed me, but sometimes I think the security guards are watching me a bit closer than the rest of the kids in the hallway. It's hard to tell.

"I've got to go," I say. "History test, see you."

"Late."

On the way to class I go by a group of Goth kids standing by the Spirit Wall. They talk shit as I walk past but the last thing I need is another trip to the office so I block it out and think happy thoughts. This is something I get told once a month at Gold Star Siblings: "Think happy thoughts." Like it's Peter Pan or something. My counselor, Marci, tells me this all the time too. It's usually at the end of my weekly one-on-one in her office downtown. We bullshit for most of the hour my parents require me to attend and then, in the last five minutes or so, she reminds me to think about things that make me happy. The way Marci explains it, it's supposed to remind me of why life is such a great thing. That my brother's sacrifice meant something. That Kyle getting blown up on the side of the road in Fuckstick Nowhere, Iraq, has something to do with keeping America free. She doesn't say that it's supposed to keep me from punching out another student, but it's what she means. Like my parents, she reminds me about how I was only able to stay in Key Club because my dad's such a pillar of the community and blah blah blah, and all that shit. Like I'm really into extracurricular activities. Like I'm doing student government and the model UN for myself and not because my mom was school valedictorian like a million years ago.

I've gotten really good at nodding my head at all the right moments. At looking like I sincerely believe every word my counselor says. Like pretending that I don't notice how she feels sorry for me. And how she's afraid of me, too. I took two years of drama, including Summer Stock Theatre. It's paying off.

Physical Education

Friday night after my parents go to sleep I sneak down to my car and drive over to the park by Kari's house and call her on my cell phone.

"Yeah?" she says. She's whispering and I picture her sitting on her bed, hunched over, head tucked under a dark, hooded sweatshirt. She's so dramatic. We've been in three plays together and she's always going on about wanting to do something exciting instead of just reading about it. Instead of just standing on stage, pretending to be somebody. When I told her I needed a partner for what I was going to do tonight, she begged me to let her come along.

"I'm here," I say.

"Okay, give me a minute, my parents just went to bed." "Can you do this?"

"Yeah," she says. "How'd you manage to get away?"

"My parents conked out early; they must've drank about three bottles of wine tonight."

"What's the occasion?"

I think about my mother looking at the folded flag on the mantel. The photograph next to it of my father pinning a Ranger Tab on Kyle's shoulder, both of them grinning like idiots in the hot Georgia sunshine.

"My dad got a promotion at work or something," I lie. "They didn't stop talking about it for two hours until the merlot ran dry and they went to their room to watch TV."

"Okay, I'll be there soon."

I wait about fifteen minutes before I see the headlights of Kari's new Jetta in my rearview mirror. She parks her car, gets into my Honda, and off we go to the river. I was right, she's wearing a black hoodie and sweatpants, her hair pulled back into a tight ponytail. We look like members of some obscure all-blond terrorist group. Like an Animal Liberation Front cell, except we both bathe on a regular basis and shave our legs.

Because it's late the entrance to the river is closed, so I park down the street a few blocks.

"What about security?" Kari says as we get out of the car. "Nothing, just park rangers, easy to dodge." They're shit, spending the whole shift tooling around in their Ford Broncos, dreaming of becoming real cops someday. I hand Kari the backpack I brought for the rocks and we duck through a hole in the chain link fence that's been there forever.

It's only a short walk to the riverbank. We actually don't need to go all the way down to the water to get the rocks; there are plenty of them lying around on the sand just past the parking lot and the picnic area. We grab a bunch of round ones, grapefruit sized, easy to throw. Anything larger and we risk losing accuracy. Anything smaller and we won't do enough damage. She licks her lips and carefully selects each rock before gently placing it in the pack, like they're Easter eggs. Like they'll break if they get too close to each other. Her nails have been French manicured; they shine in the moonlight.

"What?" she says.

I look up at her face. "What do you mean, what?"

"Why are you staring at me?"

"I'm not, I. . . wait, did you hear something?"

Car sounds. Headlights in the distance, getting closer. We drop to the ground behind some bushes as a Bronco goes by. Park ranger. I watch as he rounds the corner, making his way down to the visitor's center and the nature area where I went on a field trip in the fifth grade. My class got to hold a frog and a tarantula. A long-haired guy from the university taught us about ecosystems.

"Come on," I say. "Let's go before he comes back."

We jump up and run back to the hole in the fence, Kari bitching about the weight of the rocks she's carrying on her back. At the car, we drop into our seats, I key the ignition, and we're gone.

Math

One grapefruit-sized river rock can destroy one rear window of a parked automobile if thrown at the proper angle and appropriate velocity. The average replacement cost of a rear window in tonight's target neighborhood is $368. Kari and I have eight river rocks in my backpack. Over the next ten minutes, how much damage will she and I cause by driving forty-five miles per hour with the headlights out, hurling rocks through the back windows of luxury automobiles as we pass by?

From the river, I drive back through the neighborhood, scanning for targets of opportunity. The first street I find has enough cars, but too many streetlights. The last thing I need is some over-excited Neighborhood Watch member to write down my license plate and call the cops. I circle around for a few minutes, jumping from street to street, past million-dollar homes with wide, circular driveways, four-car garages, and For Sale signs with my mother's name and realty company on them.

"How about those?" Kari says, pointing towards a group of cars at the end of the block.

"No streetlight, enough room to get up to speed," I say. "Okay, you know what to do?"

"Roll down the window and toss the rock, right?"

"You have to make sure you get the right angle or you'll just hit a taillight or the trunk," I say. "Get a good arc; aim for the center of the back window."

"How do you know this?"

"Just throw it at the right time," I say. "You'll see. Get ready, here we go."

Kari rolls the window down and I turn off the headlights. I can still make out the speedometer as we get closer: thirty-five, forty, forty-five miles per hour. The first car is just up ahead. A brand new Mercedes resting against the curb like a sleeping child, a large, white sticker with the President's name on its bumper.

"That one," I say, pointing.

Kari leans out of the passenger window and hurls the rock towards the car. For a moment I wonder if she messed up. Then I hear the back window implode, followed by the car alarm's whoop whoop whoop as I hit the gas and tear away.

"Jesus," Kari says, her voice barely a whisper. "We just, I just. . . Jesus."

"I know," I say, reaching over and squeezing her arm gently. "You okay?"

She looks over and there's a light in her eyes I've never seen before.

"There's seven more rocks," she says. "Can we use all of them?"

"We can do whatever you want."

Biology

After it's over, I drive Kari back to her Jetta.

"That was great," she says. Her face is flushed with excitement. She's standing close enough for me to smell the lotion she puts on her skin.

"When can we do it again?"

She reaches up and pulls her hood down, takes out the ponytail. My heart beats like a caged rabbit in my chest as I take a strand in my fingers, brush it away from her eyes. It feels like spun silk against my skin.

"Soon," I say. "I'll let you know."

"What are you doing?" She tucks the strand behind her ear, cocks her head at me.

"Nothing, you had hair in your eyes." My hands drop like they're made of stone. "You did great tonight."

"Thanks," she says. "That was crazy. Whoever owns that Mercedes is going to shit when he. . . you know, sees all the glass. . . hey, are you there?"

She's waving her hand in front of my face.

"What are you staring at?"

"Nothing." Panic rises in my throat like sickness. Kari wipes her mouth with the back of her sleeve, looks at it, back at me.

"Is there something on my lips?" she says. "You keep looking at my mouth."

"No." My face, hot. "Nothing."

She gets into her car. "You're being weird," she says, and closes the door. "I'll see you at school."

"Wait." I knock on her window. She hits a button and the glass retracts with a whine.

"What?"

Music comes from the stereo; the car's engine hums low. A couple of blocks over someone's dog barks. Even in the dim light of the dashboard I can see how blue her eyes are.

"Nothing," I say. "Just, you know, don't tell anyone."

"Yeah, duh," she smiles. "Thanks for letting me come with you, it was cool."

I watch her drive away until the taillights disappear. Tomorrow, I tell myself. I'll let her know how I feel tomorrow.

Maybe.

I go home and crawl into bed. I dream of car alarms, broken glass, and Kari's mouth.

First-Person Shooter

The M16A4 service rifle, 39.5-inches long, 8.79 pounds. Maximum effective range, area target: 800 meters. Maximum effective range, point target: 550 meters. You can hit ten out of ten head shots from 500 meters on the Known Distance range in high wind. You are an Expert marksman, a hunter of men, a killer. A United States Marine. Born-to-fight-trained-to-kill-ready-to-die-but-never-will! Sir yes Sir! This is your War Face. This is your weapon. There are many like it, but this one is yours. This is your blood. This is your sweat. Give your soul to Jesus because your ass belongs to The Corps.

Run. Up the hill. Back down. Back up. Again and again and a-fucking-gain until your lungs burn and your quads feel like rubber. Sergeant Czerzinski runs alongside of your sorry ass without any discernible effort, screaming, "Get up my fucking hill!" and "You worthless piece of shit, why don't you die? Why don't you just fall out of this run and cry like a little fucking girl because this hill is just too goddamn hard for you?" The Marine in front of you pukes all over the front of his t-shirt. His step doesn't falter. He doesn't quit. Marines don't quit. Ever. You can't quit in combat. What if it's hot? What if you're tired when the enemy attacks your position? There is no "time out" in war. No second place. You know this because the sergeants have told you. The sergeants who have gone and fought and returned from their wars. The ones that you look upon with fear and admiration. The ones who have killed for their country and brought back stories and medals and scars.

CH-46 Sea Stallion. Twin rotors. Looks like a giant banana thump-thump-thumping along in the sky with you and your team in its belly. Metal and skin. Oil and sweat. The pilot drops low over the waves of Kaneohe Bay, thirty feet off the deck, navigating with night vision goggles in the early morning dark. Check your equipment for the hundredth time since getting on board. Rifle, harness, ammo, IR strobe, emergency life vest, fins, knife, check, check, check. Now slow and hover, the copter's back door opening like a giant mouth waiting to spit its cargo into the sea. Stand up and look at the other seven men in your team before lining up in the doorway. The Marines look like demons in the red light of the 46's interior. Everyone has their war paint on: light and dark green streaked over faces and necks. Your team leader, Sergeant Czerzinski, a massive, power-lifting bastard, has written "Fuck" on one cheek and "Kill" on the other. Veins the size of fingers rise and fall in his neck as he chews his gum. He steps to the back of the bird, looks over the edge, smiles at the crew chief strapped safely into the doorway and steps out into the night. You follow.

Drop. Drop. Drop. Splash.

Feet first into the cold water. Kick hard for the surface. Breathe. Swim away from the area before everyone else drops on top of your head. The instructors at the Scout Swimmer's School drove the point home: rotor blade vibrations over the ocean drive sharks into a feeding frenzy. Maybe it's true, maybe not. You don't want to find out. Reach down to the snap link on your harness. Get fins. Put them on over your scuba boots. Where's the sergeant? Where's the team? There. Link up. Tread water. Grab hands and count like children: One-two-three-four-five-six-seven and you make eight. All set? Let's go.

Practice, practice, practice. The more you sweat in peace, the less you bleed in war. All you do is sweat. All you've seen is peace. Everyone's going but you. You want to go. You want to stay. Go. Stay. Go.

Dollar beer night at The Shack in Kailua. Too many Marines, not enough girls. Try to wedge your way in close to a brunette tourist from the mainland almost sitting by herself at the bar. The conversation goes along predictable lines:

Her: Smile, laugh, toss hair, drink, drink, look around the room, laugh, ask why you're a Marine.

You: Smile, joke, drink, drink, show tattoos, look around the room, joke, lie.

Survival training. No food for days. You're taught how to skin and cook a rabbit in the field. Sergeant Czerzinski is in charge of this period of instruction. You and the other Marines each get a bunny and are told to hold it close to your chest. You are ordered to take a knife and slit the throat of your rabbit.

The sergeant says, "Hold it upside down so that it will bleed out faster." When the Marines hesitate he laughs at them. He looks at them in disgust.

"You love this bunny?" he asks. "You can't kill it now that you've been holding it all this time?"

The Marines are quiet, staring.

"That's just emotion you're feeling," he says. "Just bullshit. Now, take that knife in your hand and cut that fucking bunny's throat. Kill that goddamn thing. Fuck your feelings. Fuck feeling sorry for something. You want to survive in combat, you squash that shit right fucking now, you read me?"

In unison, "Yes, sergeant."

"You can't kill a goddamn bunny, how the hell are you going to kill a man?"

You grab the rabbit by its ears, pull back, slash the entire neck open. Blood gushes out warm over the blade, your knuckles, the dirt at your feet. You hold it upside down and listen to its breath get slower and slower until the rabbit stops moving and everything is very still.

"Right now," Czerzinski is saying, "right now, somewhere in the world, your enemy is training to kill you. He might be a trained soldier, or a teenager with a bomb strapped to his chest, or an old man with nothing to lose doing what some fucked up country tells him to do. You need to be able to kill any of them without hesitation, without mercy. Without doubt."

Your mother sends a birthday card. She says how proud she is. She writes about your little brother, who never takes off the USMC t-shirt you sent him. She says that he runs around the house playing war. He wants to shave his hair just like yours but she won't let him. She worries about you. Be careful, she writes. Be careful.

Your unit goes on float. Six months at sea on an amphibious assault ship, sailing in circles, waiting for something to happen. Pushups on the flight deck, swabbing decks, laughing at sailors for not being as tough, for not being Marines. You go to the Philippines and the battalion commander orders your unit to spend an entire Saturday afternoon rebuilding a Catholic orphanage while PR flacks take pictures for Stars and Stripes. That night, you go into town and pay five bucks to take a teenage girl into the back room of a bar. This girl, she says that she only works there part time to pay her way through college. She says she loves American movies and rock and roll and then she goes down on you and doesn't say anything more. Three days later your ship leaves and you watch the sunset over the Sea of Japan in an explosion of pink and orange. It is the most beautiful thing you have ever seen.

Midnight in the Indian Ocean. The platoon sergeant wakes everyone up. "Get out of the rack," he says. "The CO is coming through with an announcement." Your platoon sleeps stacked from deck to ceiling in bunks like coffins. The Marines stand, pissed off and bleary eyed, waiting for the skipper to make his appearance. The rumor mill is in full effect. Surprise inspection, some think. More fuck-fuck games, others say, more bullshit. What is it now? Finally, he arrives. Fresh shave, starched uniform, Academy ring like a door knocker on his hand and the First Sergeant dogging his heels like a porter.

"At ease," says the First Sergeant. "Listen up."

The CO tells the Marines that shit has gone down and they're going in to secure an American embassy. He uses words like "Noncombatant Evacuation Operation." He says, "The balloon has gone up" and "This is not a drill." He tells the junior officers to meet him in ten minutes for a briefing, and that this is what you're all here for.

Czerzinski looks over at you. "Stick with me, you skinny fuck," he says. "You'll be just fine." He sits down on a rack and starts sharpening his knife.

You make it to the head before throwing up your dinner.

It looks the same coming up as it did going down.

On the flight deck, surrounded by helicopters, the heat is a living thing. You are a hundred miles off the African coast. Sergeant Czerzinski orders your team to take their dog tags off and tie one to each boot, down low, between the tongue and laces. He explains: "You've only got one head but two legs. If an RPG hits you in the chest there won't be enough left for anybody to identify."

He says, "You need teeth for dental records."

He says, "We may find one of your boots a few hundred feet away with that dog tag in it."

You're in a helicopter again, coming in low over the ocean and across the sand. The embassy is a small, cement building squatting in the distance surrounded by razor wire and burning tires. It is hot hot hot and the world smells like gun oil, sweat, and fear.

Riding in the belly of the copter, you discover that fear has an actual taste. Acrid, metallic, copper, sour, it is all of these and none at the same time. You are learning your first lesson of war: that this fear is real. This fear is yours. It has become part of you and you will carry it in one form or another for the rest of your life.

Your mind spins in circles as you hear small arms fire pinging against the skin of the aircraft. You hold your rifle against your chest, muzzle down, fingers squeezing the stock, knuckles white. Czerzinski looks over at you and laughs. He's holding something out to you in his massive hand, gum, but you shake your head. All you can think of is how thin the aircraft is and then there's another blast against the bottom of the bird and everything shakes.

"Well, ladies," Czerzinski says. His voice is loud enough for everyone to hear but you swear he's speaking only to you. "This is where you earn your stories."

The bird lands and you hit the ground running. Everything is in slow motion as you head for the edge of the LZ with the rest of your team and throw yourself onto the dirt. You're too close to the others. Everyone is bunched up. Clusterfuck. One grenade and you all go. Czerzinski is everywhere, shoving people away and pointing, yelling,

"Spread the fuck out!" or something like it. You roll away and make for the bushes. No rocks, no trees. No hard cover anywhere. Hide and seek, just like elementary school. More small arms fire and you hit the deck. The ground becomes your lover. Crawl on your belly. Feel the dirt and weeds and grass as you dig your way through the brush. Artillery falling now like the End of Days. Ours? Theirs? Getting closer? You can't tell. Clutch your rifle and pray to get out alive. Hope that no one can see you crying. Look for the other Marines.

See the captain's hand signal: Advance. Get up and run with your team towards the embassy. Your job: secure the perimeter. Run and pray. Run and pray. Say "fuck" as loud as you can. Hit the wall. Face outboard. The shelling stops, the small arms fire remote now, distant. The loudest sound is your breathing. You lay on your belly again waiting to shoot anything that moves towards you. Silence. You wait some more. You want to shoot. Why isn't there anyone to shoot? More helicopters land. More Marines. They are everywhere now. Somewhere behind you, on the other side of the embassy wall, the ambassador is being escorted out of the building. Somewhere, your CO is getting his picture taken by an embedded reporter for today's news cycle. Outside, with your team, you wait and wait and wait. No one will ever know your name.

You ride the bird back to the ship. Your team made it back without any injuries. There's a rumor that someone in second platoon got hit, head shot, never saw it coming. Others say it's bullshit; everyone on the raid is fine. Sergeant Czerzinski wants an ammo and equipment check. You pull out your magazines and stare: they're all full. You didn't fire a single shot. You watch Czerzinski as he counts his few remaining rounds out into his upturned helmet. The muscles in his forearms pop and dance and you wonder how you and he can be part of the same species. You are the fish crawling up onto the shore, learning to breathe air for the first time. He is the evolved creature you will someday become, and this fills you with a mix of horror and excitement. You are covered in dirt and sweat and somewhere in the back of your mind you realize that this place, these people, are starting to feel like home to you.

A year later Czerzinski gets into a bar fight while on liberty in Waikiki. He kills a tourist with his bare hands, deserts the Marine Corps, and vanishes. Some say that he killed himself shortly after the fight. Others, that he went back home and snuck into Canada where he works at a car wash in Toronto. Your favorite rumor is the one where Czerzinski joined the Foreign Legion. You can picture him, shaved head, white kepi blanc, and the desert all around him. He would no longer be the man you knew. He would have changed his name.

Goodbye, Goodbye

The baby on the couch looks like he's sleeping. Wrapped in a white blanket, eyes closed, I almost believe that he'll wake up if I touch him. Then I see the pink bubbly foam around his tiny lips, the bluish-white of his skin, and I know that this is real. I pull off my latex gloves, kneel alongside the couch, and peel away layers of blanket until the body is exposed. Motionless in folds of cotton, he looks like he's resting in the center of a large white beautiful rose.

I reach over and get my camera out of the evidence bag. "Take some pictures of him like that first, then we'll turn him over," Billy says. He goes back to his phone and continues the conversation with Sheriff's Homicide.

I snap two photos, checking the lighting and angle of each shot. Winnie-the-Pooh smiles back at me from a tiny jumper, still, too still, against the baby's chest. "Billy, you want to hold him while I take some of his back?"

Billy nods at me, still talking to Homicide.

"Yeah. . . Uh huh," he says. "No, no obvious signs of trauma. Yeah, SIDS. . . right, sure, it's Billy Robeshaux. . . just like it sounds: R-O-B-E-S-H-A-U-X . . . no, Louisiana, couldn't you tell from the accent?"

I look around the room while Billy continues his conversation. I try to pay attention to everything he does, try to remember the protocol for Sudden Infant Death Syndrome. As the senior investigator, it falls on Billy to contact whatever Homicide squad has jurisdiction and let them know what we've got. I've seen horrible things in the few months I've been with the coroner's office: ODs, homicides, multiple-car pile ups on the freeway.

This is my first infant.

The body looks small, but probably within the normal range for a three-month-old. The sheriff's deputies who were first on the scene are all large men. Shaved heads, moustaches, military-looking uniforms. The same uniform I wore up until my transfer went through. These same men, they're busy in other parts of the house now. They're taking fingerprints, collecting evidence: powder blue blankets, baby bottles, a teddy bear. Anything to keep themselves out of the room with us and the work we have to do.

When Billy and I showed up at the house there was already a sergeant on scene, standard in any case where there's a body. He looked at us in confusion at first, taking in our button-down shirts and slacks, our lack of obvious identification. Billy had been doing this for so long he didn't even wear his gun anymore.

I showed the sergeant my Coroner's office badge and his face changed. I could actually see weight lift from his shoulders, his posture soften, relax, when I told him who we were.

He led us to an old, brown sofa with spots here and there where the stuffing was starting to escape. There was a catalog on the table a few feet from the sofa, some empty soda cans, a remote control. A small white cocoon lay on the cushions with a spot of pink soaking through the soft cotton blanket that covered the baby's mouth.

We stood there for a moment. I didn't realize how quiet it was until the sergeant spoke, startling me.

"My deputies moved it, uh, the baby, I mean, from the bedroom where they found it."

The sergeant gestured with his arm, showing the disposable CPR masks on the floor, two pairs of balled up latex gloves next to it.

"They did what they could, but it was too late before they even got here."

He stared at the floor, the walls, me, anything but the tiny bundle on the sofa.

"The marks on the carpet are from where my deputy pushed the table back so he could, uh, so he could lay the, uh, body down on the couch."

"Boy or girl?"

I would know in a minute, but I found myself delaying as well. I could see a small shock of black hair poking out from the top of the cocoon.

"Boy," he said. "His name is Jake. Was Jake. I didn't, uh, I didn't get his last name, hang on, my deputy's got it. He's talking with the parents outside, getting their statement."

He left the room. He wouldn't return until we were done conducting our investigation.

Billy rotates the body ninety degrees onto its side. The baby is wearing a long-sleeved jumper that snaps over a diaper. His legs are bare. The term onesie pops into my head, unbidden. It's a onesie, not a jumper. Billy unsnaps the bottom of the outfit and lifts it up to the baby's neck, exposing a deep, purplish mark along the child's back. I take another photo. The mark looks like a bruise. His heart hasn't been pumping for several hours and gravity has caused the baby's blood to pool into the lower portions of his body.

"Positional lividity," I say.

Billy presses his gloved fingertips against the purple discoloration on the boy's skin. Where he touches, the skin goes white and then darkens again when he stops pressing against it.

"Blanching, too," Billy says. "How long ago did his parents find him?"

"I don't know. The sergeant went to get some info from the deputy who got here first and took the parent's statement. Five, six hours?"

Billy is not a big fan of estimating time of death. He explained to me during my initial training that, unlike in the movies or on TV, time of death can only be predicted in the field with very broad strokes. Ten or twelve hour strokes, in fact.

"Call it, oh, less than twelve hours or so."

He lays the baby back on the couch and grabs the child's jaw, attempting to wiggle it back and forth. It doesn't move. "Rigor is set in his jaw." He continues the exam, his hands huge next to Jake's body as he methodically works his way down, wiggling the tiny arms and legs as he goes. "Wrists and ankles too. Yeah, 'bout twelve hours."

I make notes on my clipboard. After a person dies, the muscles start to tighten up. First the jaw, then the extremities. Wrists and ankles. Outside in. The rest of the body goes from there. It takes about twelve hours for rigor mortis to fully set in an adult. Twelve hours after that the body starts to relax again as the tissues continue to decay. For infants and small children the process is quicker.

"Take his diaper off," Billy says. "We need a complete set of photos for the report."

He reaches over and takes the camera from me. I put my pencil down and pull back the tape holding the diaper on. Little dinosaurs dance around the waistband. I stare for a moment, realizing that this is the last diaper this baby will ever wear. Last night was his last bedtime. What was that like for his parents? Did they get him ready for bed like always? Put on a fresh diaper. Feed him. Rock him to sleep. Lay him down.

Wake up this morning to a quiet home.

Did they wonder why he was quiet all night? Were they happy because they finally got a good night's sleep? When they went to the crib, what did they do when they saw his lips frozen in a doll's tiny pout? Did they scream? Did they stare in shock, trying desperately to deny what their eyes were telling them?

I pull back the tape, open the diaper, and stop. Billy sees me staring.

"You okay?"

"Yeah, it's just. . ."

"What?"

"Nothing."

Billy looks at me. I'm still holding the diaper, motionless. "What is it?"

I'm not listening. I'm looking at the baby. At Jake. I'm remembering my wife's face the night we found out that her birth control pills weren't 100 percent effective, like we used to joke about when we started dating. I'm remembering our conversation, how excited we both were. Taylor thought about it all the time, kept lists of names, picked out colors she wanted to paint a nursery. I bought diapers, stuffed animals, a crib. I drove her to the hospital in the middle of the night when she woke up bleeding. I remember waiting in the ER. The magazines I flipped through but couldn't read. The way Taylor agreed with me when I said everything would be all right and how that didn't keep her from crying the entire time. I'm doing addition in my head. This baby, I realize, he's about how old ours would be. Would've been. If Taylor hadn't miscarried. If we could have saved it. This baby, his hair is the wrong color, but his age is just about right.

The room is very quiet and all I can see are the cartoon characters on the diaper. The closed eyes. The small chest not going up and down. His parents wrapped him well before putting him to bed. Snug and tight and safe. Even through my gloves, I can tell that he's still warm.

"His diaper's dirty. Someone should change him."

Billy puts the camera back in the bag, looks over at the small remainder left in the center of the diaper. "It's okay," he says. "It's not going to affect the exam."

"No," I say. "I should change him."

"It's okay." Billy puts a hand on my shoulder. "Look at me, hey, look at me."

"You can't leave a baby in a dirty diaper." I turn towards Billy in slow motion, the details of his face in sharp relief against the white walls of the living room. His brown crew cut. His graying goatee. It's so quiet I can hear the blood pumping in my ears.

"It's okay," he says. "We've got enough for now. We'll let the docs do the rest."

I tape the diaper back up and re-bundle Jake the way he was when we got here. The way his parents laid him down to sleep last night. Gently, I brush a lock of hair from his forehead and try not to imagine what an autopsy will do to a body this small.

The sergeant is back.

"Your van is here," he says. "I told him to wait outside for a moment before bringing the gurney in."

"Okay, thanks," Billy says. He stands up and puts the evidence bag over his shoulder. "Your Homicide guys on the way?"

"Yeah," the sergeant says. "They'll be here in about fifteen minutes to interview the parents. Ask them what the baby had to eat last night, how they laid him down, were there any stuffed animals or pillows in the crib. The usual questions."

"Where are they?" I hear someone say from very far away.

It takes a moment before I realize that it's me.

"Outside. Grandparents and relatives and neighbors too. Lots of people. Your transport guy didn't seem like he was looking forward to going past all of them with the body."

"Well tough shit," Billy says. "That his job. I'll go get him."

"No," I say. "Wait."

"What?"

"I'll just carry him."

Billy stops in the foyer, his hand on the doorknob. "You sure?"

I tighten the blanket around the baby, pick him up, and place him against me. He looks like he's sleeping on my shoulder. I put my sunglasses on and step to the front door.

"We don't need the gurney," I say. "He's just a baby."

The weeks following the miscarriage I watched as my wife drew further and further away from me. She stopped eating, lost weight. She was vanishing in front of me. She worked days, I worked nights. She went to counseling while I slept the day away. Conversations reduced to tepid I love yous in the doorway as we passed each other on our way to and from work, our marriage slowly being reduced to walk on roles in each other's lives. Finally, she told me that if things kept going the way they had, she'd leave.

"I love you," she said. "But I don't want to live like this anymore. I can't."

I said I'd transfer to the first dayshift opening at the department if she'd stay. She agreed, but only if I went to counseling with her. I said yes, and when the Deputy Coroner opening came up, I put in my papers.

I open the door and walk down the driveway, through a gauntlet of crying relatives and consoling neighbors. When they realize what

I'm holding some of them get very quiet. Others start crying even louder, grabbing onto each other, pointing at me as I walk by. I don't stop, don't slow down until I get to the transportation van where a tall, thin man in a white shirt and black clip-on tie holds the back door open.

"Shit," he says when he sees what I'm carrying. "I don't have any bags small enough."

"It's okay."

"No, I mean, what am I supposed to do?" He looks around the inside of the van for a moment, rummages through a cardboard box full of large, white plastic bags that zip down the middle. In his frustration, he sends a pile of identification tags and biohazard labels onto the pavement between our feet. Name. Race. Contaminants.

Date of birth.

"It's okay," I say. "We'll figure it out."

"I'm sorry, it's just that nobody told me it was a—"

"I know."

He looks inside the van again, at his hands, his shoes, back at me.

I feel like I should offer him more, like I should say something to him, but there's nothing there. I feel like I'm watching this happen to someone else. Like it's not me holding this baby in my arms, this tiny bundle of cloth and skin and hair that's getting colder the longer I stand here. It's not me. I'm squeezing all of this into places I didn't know I had and if I open my mouth to say anything more I'm afraid I won't be able to contain it all and I can't do that. I have a job to do.

Two weeks after I started working at the Coroner's office my wife and I had a funeral for our child. It was the counselor's idea. She said that my wife and I were holding on to our grief and we needed to let it go if we were ever going to have a chance to move on. She said that my wife needed to say goodbye, and that I did too. I played along to make my wife happy, but I wasn't really comfortable with the idea. There was never a birth, how could there be a funeral? I told myself that I'd already moved on. I just wanted to forget. We drove to the ocean and my wife brought a tiny jumpsuit she'd bought that we buried in the sand. I stood and watched as she knelt down on the beach, whispering something lost to me in the sound of sea and wind. She fell asleep on the drive back to the city.

I never asked her what she said.

The attendant holds out his arms for the infant. Ignoring him, I move past and cradle Jake in my arms for a moment, as if I were getting ready to feed him a bottle, lay him down for a nap. I start to lower him and hear soft crying behind me. Someone touches my shoulder.

I turn and a young couple is standing there. Thick sweaters, the cold air turning their breath to steam. The woman is being held upright by the man, her eyes raw and blotchy from crying. She leans in, trying to look at what I'm holding in my arms.

"We're Jake's parents," the man says. His eyes are tiny behind a pair of thick lenses. "We didn't know if it was okay to come over, but the sheriff, he said . . ." His voice fades as he looks down at his son.

I just stare, hiding behind my sunglasses, afraid to speak.

"We just . . . " He looks at the ground.

"We just wanted to say goodbye," the woman finishes for him. She clings to her husband's arm and looks as if she may collapse at any moment.

"Of course," I say.

I lift my arms and hold the baby up to them, pulling the blanket away from his face so that his parents can get a better look. His mother leans down and kisses Jake's forehead, her hand shaking as she touches his cheek. She turns away, sobbing, and collapses on her husband's chest.

"Thank you," her husband says, his voice breaking.

After they leave I will place the baby gently onto the gurney as if it were his crib. Like he's only asleep, safe, wrapped in his blanket a dinosaur diaper. I will help the attendant strap Jake down for his trip to the morgue. We will pick the tags up off of the street, put them back into their box, and close the doors.

But right now the world is quiet and still. Right now, a father is touching his son's face for the last time. He is leaning down and kissing a baby's closed eyes and telling him "I love you."

Right now, if someone passed by on the street—someone who didn't know what the white van was for and didn't see the gurney and Jake's crying parents—this person might think this was a happy-family moment. To this person, I could've been a man showing off his new baby to his friends. I could have been the proud father of a new son.

I could have been.

Pugilist

The grass I'm lying on is wet and hasn't been cut in several weeks judging by its length. There's a small bug slowly crawling across one long, flat blade and I watch, fascinated by the fact that something could move so carefully, so unaware of the chaos all around it. This insect lives contently in a universe of its own.

I am vaguely aware of movement behind me. I sense, rather than hear, people shouting from above me. I pay no attention; I am happy to watch the bug make its way through its little world. Everything is quiet. Still. Like the world is holding its breath for one small moment.

Behind the bug the background is a blur; my glasses were knocked clean off of my face with the first hit Marco landed. I can only focus a few feet in front of me. Now, lying on my stomach in the grass beside the bus stop, the morning dew seeping through my coat; I am content to lie here in this sudden and surprising silence for the rest of my life. No more teasing. No more going to the bus stop and waiting in fear to see if Marco is going to walk to school or ambush me near the oleander bushes at the intersection where the other kids wait for the bus. A small gallery of children that has become a loyal audience for my daily hazing.

Last week Marco was sick and didn't come to school and the other kids were actually disappointed that I was left alone. I made a joke about it, the first step on a long journey toward a sarcastic and self-deprecating sense of humor. "Sorry guys," I said. "No show today." I smiled at them like we were all buddies.

Buddies.

These kids who had never once helped me out while I was pushed around the street like a rag doll. Never ran and got an adult from the neighborhood when this bully, this giant kid who was old enough to be a sophomore in high school but had failed so many grades he was still in middle school, pounded me day after day.

They are bored.

And I am the show.

And this is the way of my world.

And today I have had enough. Today, I am finally tired of sneaking back into my house without my mother seeing another black eye, split lip, or random abrasion that I try to explain away as a playground injury.

A particularly rough game of touch football at PE.

A bathroom door that swung open at an inopportune moment.

But never a bully.

My mother will not know what to do about a bully.

Her idea of how to handle things will be to report it to the school. To call the sheriff's department and file a complaint. Worst of all, to go to the bully's house and talk to his parents in an attempt to "sort things out."

Things that will only make my life worse. My teasing more intense. The image of my mother holding my hand and standing next to me at the bus stop with the other kids, this image, it's beyond horrible.

And she'll do it too.

I secretly confided in my stepfather, a career military man who, although not a great thinker by any stretch of the imagination, had a certain masculine philosophy that seemed appropriate at a time like this.

"You've got to fight this asshole," he told me one night after I admitted that my cut lip was not from getting hit in kickball.

I blinked in astonished surprise.

"Red," I said (He was Red to everyone who knew him. I didn't find out his real name for years. I'm not even sure my mother knew it when she married him). "This guy is huge. He's fifteen or something."

"Get a stick," he said.

I just blinked again.

"Or a rock, or a brick, whatever," he said. "What I'm saying is, get an equalizer. If the guy is bigger than you, get something to take away that size advantage. It doesn't matter how big a guy is, if you bash is head in with a stick, he's gonna go down."

"Something like a knife?"

"No. Never ever use a knife." He was adamant, and I remember thinking that this was odd. What could be a greater equalizer than a knife?

He went on. "And if he tries to use a knife, just tell him you're going to take it away from him."

The idea of me and my skinny body telling anyone that I was going to take a knife away from them seemed absolutely ludicrous, but I didn't mention this to my stepfather.

"What I'm trying to tell you is, even if you get beat up, it's better than being afraid to go to school. It's better to fight your enemies than to run away. Don't ever run away from trouble. Be a man and fight for yourself, or you 'll never be able to look yourself in the face."

This was not only the longest piece of advice Red ever gave me, it was also one of the most profound.

It's also how I ended up on my belly on the side of the road.

Another Northern California weekday. Forty degrees or so, light fog, and a pack of twelve-year-olds waiting for the bus in their Lacoste polo shirts and Levi's Jeans. I arrived in a pair of blue, threadbare corduroy trousers (one of four I owned) with very visible hem marks from where my mother lowered them at the start of the school year. This was her way of saving money. Buy pants that were several inches too long for me and then just "let them out" as the year went on. As a child my body grew up, not out, and I was able to wear my clothes for as long as my mother was willing to patch up the knees and elbows of my middle school wardrobe.

I made my way to the bus stop each morning, the corduroy zip-zipping as I walked down the hill towards the intersection below my house. No one else wore pants like mine. The other kids had designer labels and shopped at the mall for their clothing, and they weren't hesitant to let me know it.

Marco began picking on me at the beginning of the school year and I never found out why. I was a small, skinny kid, but that was hardly unusual at my school. I wore glasses, but this too was not unique. I was poor, but so was he. If I was going to psychoanalyze the situation, I'd say that he was beating up on me in order to fit in with the other, more affluent kids in the neighborhood, only he wasn't. Marco treated me like shit everyday he was there, but made no effort to talk to the other children at the bus stop. Even at school, he hung out by himself. Occasionally, someone would report that he was "smoking weed" with some older kids from the high school out behind the large dirt circle that served as the school's track and field course. But never was it apparent that his punishment of me led to any sort of social advancement.

Marco was huge for seventh grade. Not only had his parents started him late in an attempt to "make him bigger for sports," a not entirely uncommon event in my neighborhood, but somewhere along the way he had seen fit to fail a grade or two. Thus, at fifteen years old he towered over the rest of the kids waiting for the bus like an ogre. He couldn't have looked more intimidating if he tried. He was the perfect bully; straight from central casting. His hair was cut, if it could be called that, into a shaggy, jet black mullet that perpetually hung in his eyes. He wore an olive drab fatigue jacket year-round, beat up and dirty with US Army tapes still above the pocket, blue jeans stained with motor oil, and black motorcycle boots that he stuffed his enormous feet into. He looked like a cross between a heavy-set Joey Ramone and a Mexican wrestler and he scared the shit out of me.

But today I have had enough.

Today, when Marco pushed me at the bus stop, I turned around and hit him in his eye as hard as I could. I had to stand on my toes to do it, or maybe I just jumped up when the time came, it's not really clear anymore. I'm not sure what I thought would happen. In all of the movies that I'd seen, the bully went down like a stone when the victim finally stood up to him. I imagined Marco clutching his eye, collapsing on the ground in pain. Perhaps, in my more dramatic pugilistic fantasies (and there were, admittedly, several of these) blood spurted forth and my attacker permanently lost the use of his eye.

Of course, none of these things happened in real life.

In real life, Marco took a small step back and gave me a surprised look.

Then he threw me to the ground like a rag doll and began kicking the shit out of me.

Somewhere during the journey from standing erect to huddling in a fetal position on the ground my glasses flew off. I could feel kicks hitting my ribs and shoulders as I lay there, but also something else.

Relief.

I had stood up to Marco, and now, in my seventh-grade logic, he would see that I wasn't going to take it anymore and leave me alone. He wouldn't have any choice; bullies don't pick on kids who stand up for themselves. This was the irrefutable law of every television After School Special.

Faintly, in the distance and between the kicks, I can hear a low rumbling noise.

Salvation.

Delivery from pain.

The School Bus, hallowed be thy name.

The one rule held amongst all suburban children, regardless of their social status, was that all mayhem stopped when grown-ups arrived. Especially teachers or other school employees. The bus was no exception.

The blows stop and I hesitantly get to my feet. I can see a big green Marco-blur moving towards the intersection where the other children are forming an orderly line. I can feel hot salty tears covering my face that I don't remember crying. I am waiting for my face to swell up, my legs to give out. For someone to tell me that my nose is covered in blood.

None of this happens.

The show is over.

It's time to go to school.

Someone touches my arm.

A girl that I've never seen before is handing me my glasses. They're wet, and one of the arms is bent, but they are otherwise unharmed. I stammer out a thank you but when I look up she is gone. I carefully straighten them out and place the gold rimmed teardrop shaped lenses on my face. My mother suggested these frames when I started wearing glasses a year earlier because they "looked like something a motorcycle rider would wear." My guy who lives across the street from me is a motorcycle rider. He spends all day working on his bike in the front yard, shirtless in faded jeans. Old, blurry blue-green tattoos cover his arms like a disease, their original shapes lost to time. Sometimes I wonder what they mean, and how this skinny, weather beaten man ended up in our moderately safe suburban neighborhood of used American cars and weekend Nerf football games.

My stepfather says he's a dirtbag.

I wipe water from my face and blink a few times to clear my eyes. My world is a bit clearer, my body starting to ache. My head still buzzes with what has just happened. The rest of the world moves on, but something in me has changed. Slight, imperceptible right now, but growing.

I walk over and stand behind Marco who is last in line for the bus. We shuffle forward, inching towards the open door of my savior, big yellow #31. I can hear offbeat tic-tic sound of the windshield wipers, like an irregular heartbeat, as it starts to sprinkle. My jacket is already soaked from the damp ground where I was tossed. There is dirt on my sleeve, and my trusty blue cords have a rip in one knee.

In what seems like a dream I grab Marco by the sleeve and lean in close so that only he can hear me. I don't know why I do this, only that I have an intense need to confirm what I feel here, now, at this moment. That things have changed. Things are different. I can feel him tense up, but I know that he won't do anything with the bus right here.

I say, "We're done now."

I say, "This is over."

I have no idea where this is coming from, I only know that it's true.

Marco turns and looks down at me, and I notice that his left eye is red where I hit him.

"Nothing's over," he says. He points a finger at his hurt eye. "If this turns black, I'm going to kill you."

"We're done Marco. It's over."

My body is shaking and I want to cry but I'm too young to understand that this is adrenaline and it's normal. I'm twelve years old and I think that I'm weak because my voice is shaking so hard that it sounds like I'm freezing to death while I stand here.

Marco faces away from me and we get on the bus. I used to worry about him picking on me during the ride to school, but not anymore. My worst fear was getting into a fight with him, and now I have. I am concerned that his eye might turn black, and that he will get mad again, but part of me also hopes that it does. A kid can say that nothing happened at the bus stop, that he didn't lose the fight, but every child knows that the kid with the black eye is the one who got his ass kicked. If people at school think that I kicked Marco's ass, that won't be such a bad thing.

I would like to say that all of the kids on the bus are looking at me differently now. I would like to say that they all have a new respect for me that wasn't there before, but I can't. I am still the poor kid who shops at Woolco for his school clothes and has patches on the knees of his corduroy pants. I am the one who wears polo shirts with a tiger on the pocket instead of an alligator or a man riding a horse. I am the one whose mother trims his bangs once a month and calls it a haircut.

I am the one who hit Marco in the face and gave him a (possible) black eye.

The bus driver (who also looks like he might be a motorcycle rider from time to time) gives Marco and I the once over and then shuts the door.

"You want to sit up front behind me kid?" he says.

There is a long moment where the only sound in the world is my breathing and the Steve Miller band singing "Abracadabra" from the driver's radio bungee corded to the dashboard. Marco has already sat down and stares at me from a few rows back. He sits by himself, like he does every day. He looks angry, but that's the way he looks all the time, and I'm through being afraid every day.

I look back at the driver, slouched in his chair, smoothing out his wispy blond moustache. I can see a pack of cigarettes poking out of the pocket on the olive drab fatigue shirt he is wearing. There are military unit insignia and name tapes on the shirt in all of their proper places. Army units. I wonder briefly if our driver was in Vietnam but he looks too young. I am only twelve and a boy and war is still something romantic and misunderstood to me, something I will later learn is fought by boys not much older than I am now.

"No thanks," I say. "I'm okay."

I make my way back to an open seat near the emergency exit, my ribs starting to throb and my glasses crooked, a stupid grin on my face.

The Distance from There to Here

Jay

“That was the turn.”

“No it wasn’t,” I say.

Nicole glares at me from the passenger seat. I pretend not to notice. On either side of us passes a blur of farmland broken up by barbed wire fences and disintegrating houses.

“Avenue 20 ½ was right there and you missed it,” she says. She holds her phone up like a talisman. Its electronic voice says “rerouting.” More farmland goes by. A woman on the radio is singing.

“Babe.” I try to sound placating without being condescending. It’s not something I’m good at. “The avenues aren’t in order out here. This is the Central Valley, it’s kind of backward.”

“It’s my uncle’s house,” she says. “I think I know where it is.”

On the other side of the windshield: miles and miles of miles and miles.

"I know you think that my entire family is white trash, but you didn't have to go with me on this trip. You could have stayed home and watched football and done whatever you wanted, but you said—"

"I don't think your entire family is white trash."

"—that you wanted to come."

I can feel her eyes burning into me. Like Lot's wife, if I look I'll turn into a pillar of salt right here in the driver's seat.

"I'm sure that the exit is right around here somewhere," I say.

This entire valley is nothing but fields and dirt, but I don't tell her this. Fuel on the fire and all that.

"Does the map say—"

"The map doesn't say shit," she says. "It wanted us to turn east a mile ago. You want to look at it?"

"I'm driving."

"That was my first mistake."

I could have stayed home. I would have been all by myself for Thanksgiving, but I was fine with that. Nicole, on the other hand, was not. No way could I stay at home alone on a Major Holiday, left to eat take-out turkey and drink beer in front of the television with no one but my Raiders to keep me company. She couldn't allow that. So, when she invited me to Thanksgiving dinner with her family, what could I say? It's not good policy to tell your girlfriend that you would just as soon stay at home by yourself as drive four hours away to eat dinner with a room full of strangers. So now here I am on Rural Route Nowhere looking for a turnoff that will put us just east of a maximum security prison. Happy holidays. You learn something new every day. Today, I'm learning what desolation looks like up close. I watch her as she stares at her phone, out the window, back at her phone. Wisps of her blond hair float in the breeze from the cracked window. Her mouth is turned down into a slight frown. She bites her lower lip in frustration and looks up at me from behind dark sunglasses. She is very pretty, and of a type that I find myself hopelessly drawn to: blond, athletic, and petite. Her looks make it easier to for me deal with the more challenging moments of our relationship. I know that's not right, but there it is.

"Quit looking at me and watch the road, I don't want you to crash my car." She makes it sound like she's angry, but a smile plays at the corner of her lips when she says this. She knows I appreciate her looks. I know that it's been a long time since anyone appreciated anything about her.

I look back at the road. Two lanes surrounded by a million acres of farmland: what am I going to crash into?

She loves this car: Honda Accord EX Coupe, V-6 engine, ridiculous horsepower, leather interior, sunroof, power everything, premium stereo, loaded. Zero-to-sixty in your driveway. I have to keep in mind that her letting me drive it is a sign of how much she cares about me. She trusts me with her automobile. It's brand new and I am the only other person who has been behind the wheel. She wants me to feel honored, to understand what this means to her. I get what she's doing, but I still think it's a bit ridiculous; it's just a car. A nice one, sure, but still just a car. This is only one of many ways we see life differently. This is only one of many reasons why this relationship won't last. Why marriage is absolutely out of the question. These unstated truths follow us wherever we go. This car, it's the first thing she did for herself after she got back from Afghanistan.

Her divorce was the second thing.

"What's that?" she says, peering out the windshield towards the horizon.

I squint into the distance at a green and white road marker. As we get closer I can make out letters and numbers: Next Exit: Avenue 20 ½.

Underneath that, in smaller letters: Corchoran State Prison.

As I make the turn my girlfriend is looking right at me, waiting. I feel like I should apologize but I'm not exactly sure what for so I try to be flip but it doesn't work.

I say, "See, I told you, it's right there."

She gives me a look that says, No shit. I might be wrong about that translation, but I doubt it.

I have an afternoon of bad holiday food and Budweiser and Chex Party Mix ahead of me, and at the end of it all another four-hour drive to get back home. To lie in a bed that isn't mine next to a beautiful woman who I cannot love the way she needs me to.

Behind me are miles and miles of miles and miles.

Nicole

He has nice hands.

It's one of the first things I noticed about him when we met. Masculine. Clean. I have this thing for hands. Sometimes, when he's not looking, I watch them on my car's steering wheel while he drives. I think of how they feel on my face, my hips. It's strange, riding in the passenger seat of my own car, but I trust Jay. I want him to know that. I want him to know that I take what we're doing very seriously.

I'm glad he decided to go with me for the holiday, even if he can't follow directions for shit. I think he's nervous. He makes these stupid jokes when he gets nervous.

I'm nervous too.

The only other man I ever introduced to my family was Sean, my ex-husband. They didn't like him. I was upset for so long because I thought they were wrong. Then I was upset because they were right.

Almost everything my family warned me about was true. I was just too young to listen to them. I spent my first four years in the Marine Corps juggling deployments while living with someone who wanted me to be his mother more than his wife before I realized what I'd gotten myself into. I was always on ship or overseas, so I had to trust Sean to take care of our house and pay all the bills himself. It made me feel dependent. It also bit me in the ass when, on the other side of the world, I received delinquent notices. I'd only graduated from high school the year before; I didn't know shit about shit. I spent all of my time working while worrying about the enlisted wives who went down to Oceanside to pick up Jarheads. And husbands. The number of spouses at Camp Pendleton who remained faithful during a deployment was about the same as the number of men who did while they were overseas: very small.

My husband wasn't one of them.

Jay is so different. He's divorced too, so we both understand where the other one is coming from. It's nice, sometimes. His ex walked out on him but he's never given me the details, not even her name. I'm not sure that I want to know them. I do know that sometimes he still hurts. When we're driving, a song will come on the radio and he'll change the station for no reason. If we go to the Gaslamp, he'll refuse to take me to certain restaurants. When I ask, he'll tell me that he didn't like the service the last time he went there, or that the food was bad, but I know it's because of her. Because they used to go there together.

I've never met her. I hate her.

Unlike Sean, Jay actually listens to me when I talk about what I want to do with my life. He's so focused on the future, it's great. My ex could never hold down a job for more than a month while I was in the Corps. When I confronted him, he told me that he couldn't adapt to being alone for months at a time. He accused me of being moody. Of having post-traumatic stress from the war. He told me that the other women didn't mean anything.

I told him I was leaving.

I didn't want to be someone's mom anymore, I wanted to be me. A woman. Myself. The way I am with Jay.

Jay

Nicole told me once that she liked to watch me sleep. "It's the breathing," she said. "In and out; you look so peaceful."

Sometimes I think about her sitting in bed, watching over me while I sleep. Wondering what I'm dreaming about. Keeping me safe with her prayers.

It's almost enough to make me love her.

When I was married I used to watch my wife sleep. I worked nights, and when I came home it was always after midnight and she'd already gone to bed. I used to take my shoes off in the living room so that I wouldn't wake her when I crossed the hardwood floors into the bedroom. I would stand there, waiting for my eyes to adjust to the darkness, watching her breathe. Then I would take off my clothes and climb into bed, wrap my arms around her, and fall to sleep as she pressed her body against me in some unconscious act of love.

In those moments, when we made love, when my face was buried in her hair and the whole world became her breath, her skin, her sweat, I secretly prayed for death. Afterwards, tangled in sheets and staring at the ceiling, I would wish for it, right there, right at that moment, because I knew the happiness I felt was temporary and that soon, it would be gone.

Later, when I knew that my wife was lying in bed with someone else, I wondered if he ever felt the same way. I wondered if she made her new man happy the way she had me, and if it was too much for him to take, like it was for me. If her breath, skin and sweat meant as much to him as they did to me.

I wondered if she would leave him too.

Nicole

It's almost noon when we finally arrive at my uncle's house. It's a little later than my mom wanted, but I don't care. After driving for four hours she should just be glad that I show up at all. I feel like I'm going to church with this sweater on but it's nice and it makes me look a little softer; the last thing I want to listen to is my mother complaining about my muscles and that the Corps is turning me into a man. Besides, Jay bought it for me for my birthday on his way home from work last month. He's always getting me gifts. He likes to do that. I've gotten more flowers in the eight months we've been together than I have my entire life. He said that he saw the sweater at the mall and remembered that I told him I wanted to start wearing more than t-shirts and leggings when I wasn't at work. I read that in order achieve great things in life you need to be able to visualize them happening to you, so I do a lot of visualization. I picture where I want to be, where I'm going. I just made sergeant before reenlisting and now I'm running classes for new Marines straight out of boot camp. It's the first time in four years that I'm non-deployable, and it's great. Usually. On weekends I take Jay to different car dealerships. Last Saturday I sat in a new Mercedes sedan parked on the showroom floor. I took my shoes off and ran my bare feet over the pedals, against the soft carpet. I looked at my hands on the wheel. Short nails, tanned skin, soft leather. I breathed deeply, savoring the mixture of my perfume and new car smell, the way the gear shift felt in my hand. A salesman asked me if I wanted to talk about financing, but I'm sure he was just being polite. I told him "Not yet." I was just visualizing, but it's not something you talk about with salespeople.

I look over at Jay in his button-down and khakis. "You look good."

"Thanks."

His outfit was my idea. Jay wanted to wear a coat and tie but I told him that holidays with my family were strictly Budweiser, not champagne. I don't think my uncle even owns a tie.

"You can go inside if you want," I say. "My mom's here already."

"I'll wait for you."

"I'm going to get the food out of the back of the car first. Maybe put some lipstick on."

Jay looks at the door to the house for a moment before turning back to me.

"It's okay," he says. "I'm good."

I decide to skip the makeup and we both get the pies out of the back of the car. I check my hair one more time in the reflection from the window. Jay and I look at each other, take deep breaths, and go inside.

Jay

A few weeks ago I drove by my old house in Pacific Beach. The house my wife and I . . . my ex-wife and I . . . the house I used to live in when I was married. Since my separation I've noticed how divorce changes language, making me find new ways to describe the life I used to have. The house was on my way home from the office and I just found myself in front of it. No. That's not true. The house and my office are both near downtown, but my route on the freeway doesn't go anywhere near it. I just went there that evening. I parked across the street in front of it and stared at my old address. A For Rent sign hung in the window. After she left, I stayed for the remaining month on the lease and didn't renew. I couldn't walk around an empty house anymore.

I got out of the car and walked up the stairs to the porch, the hollow impact of my footsteps sounding exactly like they did when I used to come home to that place every night. I looked up at the high, Craftsman roof and remembered stringing Christmas lights the year before. My wife had warned me not to break my neck, and I laughed because she was the one who'd bought all those icicle lights for me to hang in the first place. I walked to the front door, still bright red from when I'd painted it last summer. I reached out, started to turn the doorknob and froze, my fingertips caressing the cold brass. I could remember hanging my coat up in the foyer. Taking my shoes off so that I wouldn't track leaves all over the hardwood floors. I closed my eyes and pictured the way my wife used to hunch over the dining room table, her nursing textbooks scattered all around her, eyes squinting behind her glasses as she made furious notes in the margins. I remembered how I used to go to her, lean down, kiss the freckles on the back of her neck under her ponytail, and wrap my arms around her from behind. I could smell her hair, salt and sunscreen from the beach, fabric softener on her sweater. I stood on my old porch like that for a few moments, hoping, somehow, that I could open the door and find her there, still sitting at the table with her notes, waiting.

After I left the house I stopped at the mall and bought Nicole a sweater. It was her birthday. I gave it to her as soon as I got home and she never asked where I'd been.

Nicole

I haven't been in my uncle's kitchen for five minutes when I hear him boom my name from the other room. I put my pie down on the counter and almost get turned around before he wraps his huge arms around me and lifts me off the linoleum floor.

"C'mere, Nic," he says, squeezing the air out of me. "My God, it's been a long time, hasn't it?"

He puts me back on my feet and Jay reaches a hand out to steady me before I stumble in my heels. He's still as strong as ever, even though he's been retired for five years now. "Yeah, Uncle Stu," I say. "I haven't been up here since right after you stopped working at the prison."

Stu stares at Jay. He takes in Jay's shoulder-length hair, the button down shirt, the nice shoes.

"Uncle Stu," I say. "This is my boyfriend, Jason." Jay sticks his hand out.

"Nice to meet you."

Stu slowly pulls his huge hand from the pocket of jeans older than I am and shakes Jay's hand. It's a quick shake, and although Jay works out regularly there's a quick moment of concern on his face when my uncle grabs him. Stu takes his hand back, rubs it over his shaved head and motions to the fridge.

"You need a beer, Jason?"

"Sure," he says, which is the only right answer in this house. If he had asked what kind of beer there might have been trouble. Stu hands Jay a Bud and leads him into the living room with the other men. My mother and her sister are at the snack table. I cross the room to face them.

"Mom," I say, kissing her cheek. "Aunt Beth. Wow, look at all that food. Did you make that parfait?"

My mother looks over at Jay before resting her eyes on me. She smiles, but only with her mouth.

Jay

Stu looks like a drill instructor straight out of Central Casting. No hair, huge chest, looks pissed off even when he's smiling, which is never at me. He points me towards the couch and a pair of men who look remarkably like Stu minus about forty years.

"My sons," Stu says.

The first gives my hand a quick shake and says "Troy" as I sit between them. He jerks his chin towards the person on my left, "My brother, Tom," then, "It's third and goal on the five and the fucking Raiders are trying to score." I take a long pull off of my beer and put the bottle on the table next to an issue of American Rifleman. I look at Troy and Tom in their matching Cowboys jerseys, their father in a quilted red flannel shirt. I picture how stupid I must look to them in my pressed chinos, dark blue shirt, and leather shoes. I take another drink and look across the room for Nicole. I can see her in the dining room, surrounded by older women, eating snacks, laughing.

Occasionally, one of the women looks in my direction and smiles, and then goes back to talking with Nicole. These women, I hope they're giving her approving comments about me. I have never met anyone as concerned about what their family thought of them as my girlfriend. She sees me looking at her and smiles, brushes a lock of hair out of her green eyes, and goes back to her conversation.

The Raiders score and all three men groan in unison. "The hell with this," Stu says, standing. "I'm gonna get another beer. Jason?" I look up at him. "Beer?"

"Uh, no, thanks," I say. "I'm okay."

"You sure?" Stu looks at me for a moment, waiting.

"Well, okay."

"I've got to get some more out of the garage, why don't you give me a hand."

I follow him outside to the detached garage. It's gigantic. The main door is wide open and there's a huge Chevy 4x4 inside with a Harley Davidson parked next to it. A sailboat sits on a trailer in the driveway under a gray tarp. On the floor in the back corner of the garage, next to a weight bench and a refrigerator, are several cases of Budweiser longnecks.

"Nice," I say.

"Thanks. Lots of overtime."

I'm making my way back to the beer when I notice a set of ancient shelves covered with tools and sailing books. There's a vaguely triangular object on a stand next to an old wooden globe. Stu sees me looking at it and walks over.

"Do you know what that is?"

"No," I say.

"You ever do any sailing?"

"No," I say. "Just some paddle boarding here and there."

"I try to get out in the summer," he says. "Hook the boat up and make the trip to Morro Bay. It's one of my favorite things to do."

"Nicole never told me you liked to sail."

"Before I came to Corchoran I was a C.O. at San Quentin." He rubs his scalp. "I used to go out on the water every weekend."

"So," I say, "isn't this used for navigation or something like that?"

"It's a sextant," he says, handing it to me. It has a weight to it that I wasn't expecting. "Sailors used them to find their way across the ocean when there were no landmarks. They used the sun, the stars, to keep from getting lost, to know where they were."

"You use this on your boat?"

"No." Stu takes the sextant from me and returns it to the shelf. "I just like the way it looks, the history of it. I use a GPS when I go out."

I walk over to the beer and put my hands on a case. I make a move to pick it up but Stu is still by the shelves.

"You know, ever since her parents got divorced when she was a little girl, I've been like a father to Nicole." I can see his breath when he speaks. Looking past the gravel driveway I see rolling hills and a thin fog just now starting to burn off in the early afternoon sunlight.

Split rail fencing lines the countryside and the nearest neighbor must be at least a half mile away. I feel like I'm on the moon.

"I knew Sean, her ex," he says. "Yeah, I've heard stories about him."

"Well, he wasn't the brightest boy, but he tried to do the right thing."

Nicole told me this story before I moved in at the start of the summer. She'd married her high school boyfriend, joined the Marine Corps, done time in Afghanistan. She'd gotten pregnant but lost the baby early on, convinced herself that she really loved this guy, tried to make it work. When it didn't, she divorced him, reenlisted for a non-deployable instructor slot and moved on with her life.

"She's told me a little bit," I say.

"Uh huh," he says. "She told me you met at the courthouse, but she didn't tell me how. What happened?"

"Oh, well, she had jury duty."

"Right, I know that." Stu walks over to me, opens two beers, hands me one; we're going to be out here for a while. "But what were you doing there?"

"Oh, I'm there a lot," I say. "I work with attorneys, for the county."

Stu takes a drink, sets the bottle down. "Hmm, doing what kind of work?"

"Criminal law," I say. "I'm an investigator for the Public Defender's office."

"Must pay pretty nice," he says. "I hope so, for what you have to do."

"No, it's not like that," I say. "I interview clients most of the time, run paperwork around, that sort of thing. I go to law school at night. I'm not rich or anything."

"Still, that's a nice sweater you got Nic."

"Yeah, well, it was her birthday."

"And the watch?"

I try to remember why I gave her the watch. I can't. "It was just something I thought she'd like."

He looks out the open door at something on the horizon. Windmill? Cow? He stares for what seems like a long time.

"Her mother tells me you bring her flowers, too."

I finish my beer. "Yeah, so, I like to give Nicole gifts, is there something wrong with that? I would have thought that you would be thrilled that your niece is dating someone with a good job who treats her well. I'm not sure what you're getting at."

"Easy kid, easy." Stu rubs his hands together. "I'm not saying anything. I just wanted to get a look at you."

"Well, I guess you have."

"Jay, men give gifts to women for two reasons."

"Yes?"

"Either they love them and want them to be happy, want to show the woman how much they love her," he says.

"Or?"

"Or, they're compensating for something that's missing in the relationship."

He hands me a case of beer, picks another one up, and starts back to the house.

"And you're telling me this because . . .?"

"Just trying to figure out which one you are."

I can hear our footsteps on the gravel as we walk back. I've lived in a city for so long that I've forgotten just how remote you can still get in the world, and the things you notice when there's nothing to distract you.

At the door, Stu stops for a moment, turns to look at me before going inside.

"She loves you," he says.

"She told you that?"

He turns away to open the door. "She doesn't have to."

Nicole

Everyone gives me their opinion on Jay as soon as he goes into the living room with Uncle Stu. My aunt starts before I even sit down.

"He's cute, Nicole," she says. "How long have you two been going out?"

"He needs a haircut," my mother says.

My aunt dismisses her statement with a wave of her hand. She's four years older than Mom but you'd never know it by looking at her. Aunt Beth is at least forty pounds lighter and has lines in her face from smiling instead of frowning, this despite raising three boys. I am the only girl in our family.

"Who cares about his hair? What does he do for a living?"

"He's an investigator for the county," I say.

"Oh, he's a cop?"

"No, he's a civilian. He does investigations for the Public Defender's office," I say. "Interviews, paperwork, he doesn't carry a gun or anything."

"Oh, well, that's nice, I suppose," she says. "Can you make a career out of that?"

"He's going to law school at night."

This statement gets the predicted reaction from my aunt.

She tells me to snatch him up quick. My mother reminds her that we've only been dating for eight months. My aunt is nonplussed. They go back and forth while I sit there.

My aunt: "When are you going to get a ring, Nicole?"

My mother: "He's divorced."

My aunt: "Well, so, that doesn't mean anything."

My mother: "Recently . . . divorced."

My aunt pauses to refill her wine glass and I quickly hold out mine as well. If they're going to go down this route I need all the help I can get.

"How recently?" my aunt says.

I take a big swallow of white zinfandel before answering. "Actually," I say. "It's not final yet."

It's a long time before anyone speaks. Then, finally, from my aunt, "Oh, so he's separated."

"Yes, he's legally separated," I say. "Everything's been filed, it's just not final yet, that's all."

My aunt takes another drink, then I do, then my mother.

They stare at me from across the table.

"Well," my aunt says. "That's nice. He seems nice."

"Beth, you need help with that turkey?" Mom says, and they both get up from the table and go to the kitchen, leaving me with a half bottle of wine and too many questions I don't have the answers to.

Jay

A few weeks ago I finally looked at a group of photos taken last Christmas with a camera I no longer owned. It was a small file. Twenty-four pictures on a flash drive that I'd buried in a drawer and tried to forget about. It was the last Christmas I spent with my wife. I was going to throw it away. I should have. I told myself that there might be some pictures of friends that I'd want to keep, that it was stupid to just toss it without seeing what was on it first. I plugged the drive into my laptop at the office and opened the files. There she was, smiling at me from the computer screen, dressed for Christmas Eve Mass in dark green velvet, wearing the necklace I'd bought her during the weekend we spent in Costa Mesa after Thanksgiving. I was surprised at the details my memory had missed: the shade of her lipstick, how light her hair was, the fading summer tan of her skin. I put the flash drive in the glove box of my car, drove home, and forgot about it for a couple of weeks until the night Nicole brought up Thanksgiving with her and asked me where we wanted to go for our first Christmas together. The next day when I got to work I took the drive out of my car and stomped on it. Tiny pieces exploded like shrapnel beneath my feet while I clenched my fists, fingernails leaving half-moons in my palms.

Nicole

The turkey is overcooked and dry, my mom forgot marshmallows for the sweet potatoes, and from the reaction of my cousins in the living room Dallas is getting their ass kicked by whoever they're playing. But it's my family, and for the first time in my life I feel like I've got something to show them. I've got a career that's going well, I'm starting college next semester, and I've got a boyfriend who has a future and treats me nice and wants to take care of me.

We met at jury duty. I was outside by the main entrance and he was walking in with some attorneys. He was wearing a dark suit, and as he walked past me he took his sunglasses off and looked me right in the eyes. Later that morning, after I was released from duty due to my military status, I saw him in the hallway downstairs. He walked up to me and said, "Hi, I'm Jay, what are you doing for lunch?" Just like that. I've never met anyone so confident in my entire life. He was so self-assured it took my breath away. He took me to lunch and we've been together ever since.

I ran into my ex the other day. I was at Home Depot to buy some paint—Jay and I are fixing up my condo—and there he was, Sean, with his shaved head and his tattoos, unloading freight onto the floor. We talked for a little while, then I bought my paint and went home. I told him that I was living with someone now and that I was happier than I had ever been in my life. Sean told me that he knew me better than anyone else ever would because we were married. He said that no one I ever went out with would know me like he did. He said that it's only natural. He's wrong. Sean knows who he was married to, yes, but that's not me. It was never really me. I don't think he knows me at all. I don't think he realizes that, to me, he has become a stranger. Someone I would pass by without bothering to look at on my way to somewhere better.

Jay

When I met Nicole I had been falling for so long that I didn't think there was a bottom. I had reached a point where my loneliness had taken on shape and form until I no longer remembered what my life was like without it. She came into my life and made me remember that I hadn't always been that way. She is beautiful and warm and loves me, and all she wants is for me to love her back more than anything else in this world. She deserves that. But I did that before with someone else, and it almost killed me when it ended. I have learned not to give anything away that I can't stand to lose.

I watch her as she sleeps in the passenger seat, her shoes on the floor, seat reclined as far as it will go. I find my way out of desolation and back to Highway 99 South. Away from Tulare County and rolling hills and farmland and Level III prisons. Away from Nicole's family, who, unlike mine, seem to actually enjoy each other's company. My hand is still sore from shaking goodbye to Stu. After our conversation in the garage the only words he said to me were when we were leaving.

"You're going take care of her, right, Jay?" It wasn't really a question.

Nicole looks over at me, eyes half closed, and says, "I love you."

"I love you, too," I say, but I don't know what that means anymore.

Nicole

I'm ready for a new life. I'm ready to love someone again and there is so much about Jay that I really like, that I really need. When he looks at me, I know he's really seeing me, not someone else. I know, deep down, that we're not just playing house, and that someday we'll both be able to admit it. I think about how far I've come, and how far I still have to go, but it's all too much right now. I'm so tired.

Jay

She closes her eyes. I turn the radio down until I can hear her breathing, deep, slow. In and out. In and out. I watch this woman who loves me and think about the one who doesn't. This woman I don't deserve, and the one I can't forget. While she sits there dreaming I look back to the road, at the sky. It's overcast, and the fog is rolling in.

Be Mine

I spend the afternoon lying in bed next to the man I love, relaxing in the tranquil effect that good sex always has on me. I tell him about my day at the hospital, the patients, the child who needed stitches and the father of three who died of a heart attack before we could get the crash cart in place. He touches my hair, my face, my skin, and I forget about the rest of my life for a few moments. Then I get up and go home to clean up before my husband comes home.

The man I love, Mark, fits into the places in my life that John, my husband, doesn't. The places that John doesn't know about because he doesn't listen anymore when I try to tell him who I am. John wants me to be the girl he fell in love with years ago in college over a cup of coffee. The one who saw past his tough guy, former Marine façade and listened when he spoke about his service, his friends, the war. The one who carried Sartre and Camus around in her backpack with her nursing textbooks, discussing existentialism while studying emergency medicine. The painfully shy girl who watched everyone else live life while she sat still, safe behind her books. That girl doesn't exist anymore. I used to wonder what happened to her, now I'm just glad she's gone.

My lovers, in order: Matt, in the back of a car my junior year of high school. Luke, the Lacrosse player I was with my first year of college. Paul, the TA in my Intro to Philosophy class. John, my husband. And now, Mark.

Since losing my virginity I've slept with all the gospels.

It isn't that Mark is a better lover than John. Or a worse one. It's not a size thing, or the way one touches me or the other doesn't. It's that Mark listens and John doesn't anymore. It's that simple.

It's that complicated.

It's a few days later and John comes home from work late (again). After he's hung up his jacket and put his shoes in the closet I tell him that the hospital called right before he got home. That I have to work an extra shift to cover a shortage in the ER. Then I go to Mark's apartment. I don't really need to make up an excuse to leave. John doesn't ask me any questions. He never does.

At Mark's I talk about the woman who crushed her sternum in a car accident. The way the doctors all ignore me and the other nurses even though the place would fall apart if we stopped showing up and how there are days, so many days, now, where my house is the emptiest place in the world to me.

"There are times," I say, staring at the floor with my fists clenched. "Days when I'm so mad at him I could just scream."

Mark stands right in front of me. When I came over, he answered the door with his shirt off and now, in the dim glow from the streetlights outside, I can make out the hard ridges of his stomach muscles. "You can scream now, if you want," he says. "No one will mind."

"No, I mean, sometimes," I can feel my face getting hot, tears threatening. "I just wish…"

"What?"

I wish John didn't talk me out of having the baby, I want to say, but it's too much. Some things aren't meant to be shared.

Instead I lean up and kiss him, hard, and he puts his hands on my hips. There's a rattling sound as my hospital ID card, still clipped to my scrubs, hits the floor. Then we're on the bed, and his hands on my neck, my chest, my thighs. His mouth warm and wet, not letting up until I'm asking, begging.

Later, when I know John is asleep, I go home.

I strip down, take a shower and towel off all of the evidence of my infidelity. My shower has brought John out of his sleep and he lays in the bed, watching me, his eyes half closed as I put on a pair of shorts and a T shirt. I climb into the bed next to him. He puts his arm around me and pulls me close, my back touching his chest.

"I love you," he says, and I feel something sharp inside me. Guilt? If it is, it's only a small sliver, then nothing.

"I love you too," I say into the pillow.

I do. And I always will, in that small part of me that remembers the way he used to look at me in that café back in college. The way that Mark will look at me someday.

I close my eyes and dream of drowning.

Mark, weeks later, at the other end of my phone when I'm on break at the hospital:

"Tonight," he says. "I need to see you tonight."

"I can't."

"Really, I need to."

I think about the way he grabs me in bed, against the kitchen counter, the hallway. The hunger in everything he does, it drives me crazy.

I say, "You mean your body needs to."

One of the doctors overhears me as she walks by and I quickly turn away, hand covering the phone.

"No, it's not like that," Mark says. "Just stop by tonight after your shift ends."

In college, after I'd met him at a party, John took three weeks to get up the nerve to ask me out. We went to coffee at a small, rundown café near the campus that was struggling to stay alive, which is why he loved it so much. That's John, always looking for something to save. Fighting to the last breath when it's obvious that all hope is gone. It's what made him a good student then, and a good businessman now. We sat at a table on the patio and had cheesecake and drank dark coffee from tiny cups, one after the other. All of my clothing was black and John's hair was long, not from any sense of fashion, but because he'd just got out of the Marine Corps and told me he finally didn't have to get it cut every week. It was brown and unruly and hung in his eyes and I loved it. He didn't do anything to try to impress me like other guys had, and, of course, this impressed me.

We finished our coffee and cake and drove around town in his Honda listening to indie music on the college radio station. He'd seen my philosophy books and we talked about The Duality of Man and The Nature of Truth and a bunch of other stuff that he obviously didn't know that much about but I didn't stop him because I wanted to hear him talk for as long as he wanted and I didn't care what he said. I just wanted to listen. To lose myself in his words and his voice and forget where I was.

Mark lives in a loft above a Harley Davidson shop in midtown. I make my way past the front window. In this neighborhood of aging hipsters and artist lofts the sign above the garish display of leather and chrome and horsepower should read, "Enter Here for Instant Midlife Crisis" rather than, "Ride to Live, Live to Ride." Mark's door is next to the alley. I ring a doorbell that was probably installed sometime around the Nixon administration.

Mark comes down the stairs to meet me in the usual: jeans, untucked t-shirt, close cropped black hair. His mouth is turned down, almost cruel, and when I go to kiss him he turns away and starts back up the stairs.

"Make sure it's locked behind you," he says over his shoulder, like it's the first time I've been here.

His loft is done exactly the way you'd think it would be. Walls: none. Furniture: Dark, minimalist, European. Weight bench in one corner. A king-sized bed in the other. This is where we met six months ago.

It was an after party for a local theatre group. A friend of mine knew some of the actors. John was working late on a new project so he couldn't make it. I wasn't going to go at first. There had been a pile up on the freeway and I'd just worked a double-shift in the ER. Sixteen hours up to my elbows in bags of Type O and saturated bandages. I was going to go home to shower and sleep, but my friend told me that it would be fun, and that I never went out anymore. True and true. We had a great time and after an hour I noticed this ridiculously fit guy who'd been looking at me since I got there.

"Who's that?"

"That's Mark," my friend said. "He's one of the actors in the show."

"He's keeps looking over at me".

"Yes, he does. You going to keep looking back?"

Mark goes to the fridge, gets a beer, offers one to me.

"No thanks," I say, watching the veins in his arms swell as he opens the bottle. The way they do when he pins me to the bed.

I put my purse down on the table and walk over to him, white Nikes squeaking on the vinyl plank floor. I put my arms around his waist and think, not for the first time, about how much firmer his stomach is than John's. I lean in to kiss his neck but he pulls back before my lips touch skin. His cologne lingers in the space between us.

"Don't," he says. "That's not why I called you."

"Okay," I say. "Why did you call me?"

He looks out the window, takes a pull off of his beer. Opens his mouth, starts to say something, stops. His lips form a smirk, like the entire world is an inside joke only he understands. This is his trademark. His tic. It's one of the first things I noticed about him when we started seeing each other.

Two weeks after the party I was at a bar downtown with some friends. Girl's Night. John was working late and suggested that I go out and have fun. I did. We all had too much to drink and were dancing much too close to guys we didn't know and one of them tried to grab me. Did grab me, actually, squeezing my ass and pulling me close to him. I think he was going to kiss me but I never found out because suddenly someone else knocked the guy's hand away and stepped between us. It was Mark.

"Hey," he said. "It's been a long time. How are you?"

I just stared at him, the Mai Tais making it hard to remember who this person was.

Mark looked over at the Grabber, then back at me. "You know," he said. "From the after party? Mark?"

I finally caught on and hugged him just as my molester made his way back to me. He stared for a moment and I held on to Mark, squeezing him closer until the other guy went away.

"You okay?" he said.

"Yeah," I said. "Thanks for the save."

"No problem, I'll see you around."

He turned to walk away and I grabbed his arm. Alcohol, gratitude, I don't know why I did it now. I'd say it was the way he looked at me, but I'm not sixteen. He turned back.

"You want a drink?" I said.

That's when he did it: Stare, start to speak, think better of it, and smirk instead.

"Sure," he said. "Why not?"

Now I'm driving home and I've got the radio on but I don't know what the person is singing about. I'm just driving and driving and driving and somehow I know I'll end up at my house because I always do. No matter how tired I am after a shift, or how late it is, or early, I find my way home. Sometimes, I don't even remember driving. I'm just there all of a sudden. Automatic pilot. I need this skill tonight to keep me from driving off of the road into a ditch and ending up in my own ER.

A few minutes ago, or an hour ago, or whatever, Mark told me, "I can't do this anymore."

Just like that. Like some fucking soap opera, or a line in a bad movie. No preamble, just, "I need to break this off before it gets too serious."

"Too serious?" I said. "You've been fucking a married woman for six months now for fuck's sake. What's your definition of too serious?"

"Calm down," he said. "Calm down. Just let me explain."

And blah blah blah and I feel bad and Weren't we just having fun? And bullshit bullshit bullshit and so I drive and drive and drive and I can't cry because what will I tell John if I come home with a face full of tears?

"What did you think?" Mark said to me when he saw me getting upset at his loft. "Where did you see this ending up?"

Ending up? I didn't see it ending. I saw a beginning, a chance, a possibility. I saw someone who cared about what I had to say and what was important to me and I'm a fucking idiot because I saw what too many women have been trained to see in a man: a possibility, a chance, a change, a future.

Mark saw a nice ass. Mark saw someone he could fuck for a few months until he got back together with the woman he was with before he met me. The woman he told me he loved tonight. The woman who he was "taking a break" from while he used me to fill the space between.

A woman on the radio is singing. She says, Love was your great disappointment.

I pull up in the driveway and, for the first time in forever, John is home on time. I go inside and drop my bag on the couch and go to the kitchen and reach for the scotch he keeps above the refrigerator. I pour two inches into a glass and take a deep swallow, the liquor burning its way down the length of my body.

John comes into the kitchen and hugs me from behind.

"Hey, babe," he says. "What's with the scotch, something happen at work?"

"No," I say, or I mean to say, only I don't. I can't. A small, choking cry is the only sound that escapes my lips. I turn around and John holds me close to comfort me but I wish it was someone else and then he's holding me to keep me from falling to the floor because my legs don't want to work anymore.

"Hey," John is saying from somewhere else. Somewhere where his wife has always been faithful to him. "It's okay," he says. "Whatever it is, you can tell me. I'm sorry I've been so busy. I love you."

Something inside me breaks loose and I don't want to cry but I can feel my face getting hot and I close my eyes as tight as I can but the tears come anyway. My throat makes inhuman, primal sounds and I clutch John's shirt and smell his cologne, the one he's worn since school. Suddenly it's all there, flashing in the red and blue patterns behind my closed eyes. The café, our first kiss, then careers, and late nights, and the abortion, and too much work, and two people whose marriage has become Hello and Goodbye and I Love You as they pass through each other's lives. Then Mark, listening to me, making me feel like someone understood again. And making love in his loft, on the floor, in his car. From far away I hear my husband, apologizing to me for nothing he's done and I cry and I cry for who I've become and what I've done. For the stupid girl I used to be, naïve enough to think that someone could come along and save me. I cry because, even now, I still want someone to. And I hear John say, "It's okay, I'm here. I love you. Let it out. Let it all out."

"I love you."

Safety

If you are sitting in an exit row please identify yourself to a crewmember to allow for reseating if:

a) You lack the ability to read, speak, or understand the language

b) You cannot understand the graphics on this safety card

c) You told her that you loved her but she said that wasn't enough

It was the last conversation you had with her, that night, when she left and went out the door and drove off and it was raining, you think, but you can't remember exactly. Sureness isn't something that comes easy or often these days. Your doctor says you'll get used to it or snap out of it. Either way, it's not supposed to last long, this unsureness, this feeling of transition you seem to be trapped in.

This afternoon, at the airport, you went to the men's bathroom. Packed. You waited to go, fighting the urge to hop up and down on one foot like a little kid to keep from pissing your pants, watching the other men standing in front of the urinals like superheroes: hands on hips, groins thrust forward, eyes never wavering from the tile wall directly before them. When it was your turn, you too stared at the tiles, the handle, the white urinal cake resting below you. Anything you could find to avoid staring at what was going on around you, losing yourself in the monotony of everyday objects.

Now, on the plane, you fly over Texas, Arkansas, Louisiana. The world outside your window is black, black, black. You could be in space. You could be underwater.

In case of an overwater emergency, your seat cushion may be used as a floatation device. Federal Aviation Administration regulations prohibit smoking on this flight, but, goddamn, could you use one right now.

You told her you loved her, or you think you did. "Love," she said, looking over her shoulder from the doorway just before she left, the air thick with fireflies and southern humidity. Before she drove off. **"I don't know what that means anymore. I don't know if that's enough."** And what could you tell her about love?

a) Before her there was nothing. Now that she's gone, nothing again

b) That brief moment of living in between, was that love?

c) Sometimes you can feel her presence on your skin, light as breath

d) Other days, she pulls you down like gravity

When you close your eyes it's becoming harder and harder to remember her face. It's blurry now, like a smudged photograph, dark around the edges. Like the faces of the dead you saw killed in the war not so many years ago. Ever since that night, when she left, the woman who helped you keep everything together, or at least pretend to, you feel like all of the color has been washed out of the world. You probably said more to her, before she turned to leave, and after, to yourself, staring at her as she walked down the sidewalk to the car. Probably. It's not clear anymore.

"Charlie," you might have said, because that was her name. She always hated it. She said it was a boy's name. That her father had always wanted a boy, and that's how she ended up with it.

"What is it? What's—"

"I just need some time," she could have said. "Things just don't make sense to me anymore. I need to figure it out."

Of course, since that day, since she drove off, you could very well have made all of this up in your head. Filling in the blanks to explain why she left with a conversation that may never have happened. You've read about things like this happening to people. It's not, you realize, entirely out of the question.

In the event of an emergency in which a crewmember is not available to assist, a passenger occupying an exit row seat may be called upon to perform the following functions: you work, you travel, you build up thousands of frequent flyer miles. You hope for storms. You pray for turbulence so powerful it will rip the skin off of the plane and suck you out into the sky.

"I just wanted to tell you," a co-worker said the other day. "The way you're handling this, I mean, what happened with your wife, it's just, you're doing great, man. Really great."

You wondered if he was talking to the right person. If you stand still for too long, if you stop moving, working, your life starts to unravel, piece by piece. You had no answer. "Thanks," is what you finally settled on.

You are almost positive that you told her you loved her. You keep remembering inconsequential things about her, little things you can't get away from. The way she tapped her fingers when she read. How much she hated the Army, but married you anyway, then talked you into leaving, which you first hated, then thanked her for. The impossible number of flip-flops she owned, and how she wore them all year round. The pale pink of her toenail polish (not paint, Charlie corrected you once. You paint a house, she'd said. You polish nails) she wore the night of your last argument.

Please ask to be reseated if you are unable to perform one or more of the applicable functions depicted on this safety card or listed below because you:

I) Lack sufficient mobility, strength, or dexterity in both arms and hands, and both legs to:

a) reach upward, sideways, and downward to the location of the emergency exit and exit-slide operating mechanisms

b) push, shove, pull, or otherwise manipulate those mechanisms

c) reach the emergency exit expeditiously

d) she hated flying

Wait.

Actually, you have no idea how she felt about flying; the two of you never flew anywhere together. As far as you were aware, she'd never been on an airplane. Not like you, flying everywhere. First, in the military, then for work, training, seminars. Never with her. You realize, looking out the window at the darkness, at 30,000 feet of cold and black, that you'll never really know how she felt about flying. Maybe she would have loved it. Maybe she would have yearned for the feeling of escape.

Six years of marriage. Of living in the South, of North Carolina, then Florida, driving your shitty Toyota with no air conditioning and only the driver's window could be rolled down. Getting The Look on the commute home during the summer, that Zen-like acceptance of the heat and humidity that came from living in a city where the mercury didn't dip below ninety degrees, day or night, for six months out of the year. Then you and Charlie bought that car. A wagon. A horrible little compact wagon, lime green for Christsake. But the air, oh Jesus, the air on that thing. How that air worked. On summer weekends you and she would go for long drives to the ocean, turning the controller down so low you could have worn a sweater, seen your breath. Forget the gas mileage, it felt great.

II) Lack the capacity to perform one or more of the applicable functions without the assistance of an adult companion, parent, or relative

III) Lack adequate ability to impart information orally to other passengers

That last night, when she drove off mad about something you said, or money, or renting instead of owning, you can't remember the topic anymore, just that she told you, after you think you said

"Wait," and maybe, "I love you," that she said "That's not enough," and drove off in that little green wagon.

You were going to ask her what that meant when she came back. When she came back from her mom's or her sister's or her best friend's or wherever she went to calm down after the fights. You were going to apologize, like you always ended up doing, even though you usually didn't know what for. And you were going to ask, and kiss her, and maybe make love, like the two of you did sometimes after the fights. You tell yourself that this is what was going to happen. But after she left there was the intersection, and the other car running that red light, and what the police report called a "High speed 90-degree impact to the driver's door" of that ugly wagon the two of you bought. Did she have the air on that night? Was she enjoying the ice-cold breeze against her face, listening to the radio, as she drove to wherever she was going? You don't think about it that much, but when you do, you hope she did. You hope she didn't see the car coming.

Has:

a) responsibilities, such as caring for other people, that might prevent the person from performing one or more of the applicable functions

b) a condition that might cause the person harm if he or she performs one or more of the applicable functions

c) the next time you saw her was at the hospital You did apologize, all night and most of the next day, but she couldn't hear you. She lay under lights that sucked the color from her cheeks, and her lips were cold when you kissed them.

Samsara

Go to the bar. Buy a beer. Buy two. Forget that you're still holding one you bought just a few minutes earlier that you haven't finished yet. Put it down while you pay for the new ones. Open both bottles. Drink one as quickly as you can. Chase it with the other. Still thirsty. Can't taste anything. Is it the cigarettes you've been chain smoking or the acid you dropped a couple of hours ago? Can anyone in the bar tell that you're tripping? Are you tripping? The room bends. Light distorts through a filter in your mind but nothing is sinking in. Take your unfinished beer with you and leave the empty bottles on the bar. You notice a girl from across the room. She notices back. You make your way over to her through an ocean of dancing bodies and sweat as if pulled by an invisible thread. There is no conscious thought, no reason, only her smile as you find yourself standing next to her. You smile back and she says something you can't make out above the throbbing beat that surrounds you like a pulse. "What?" you say.

She moves closer, her lips next to your ear. When she repeats herself you feel her breath against your skin.

"What's your name?" Her voice is rich, melodious. "Weaver," you almost answer, because you are a Marine and Marines don't have first names, but you pause a moment and catch yourself. You tell her your name. Your old name from a time before camouflage and guns and anger.

"Paul," you say. "My name's Paul."

The girl smiles and her jet black hair shimmers but you don't know if this is from the LSD or the lights at the bar. Her smile is electric and you hope it's for you and you alone. This acid, it makes you feel like your head and your ass are connected by lightning that shoots up and down your spine. It makes it impossible for you to sit still and you hope this girl doesn't think you have ADD or some shit like that. Her hair is pulled back into a ponytail and the lower half of her head is shaved down to the skin. You notice the lotus tattoo at the nape of her neck, green and black ink against the burnt ochre of her skin. You wonder if she will know that you're three hours into your trip. You don't think she's the kind of girl who will be disturbed by a little dope, but you never know.

Buying the dope wasn't easy. You had to go to a friend of a friend who knew a guy in the motor pool who'd supposedly brought some shit back from the mainland when he'd come off of leave. You are stationed in Hawaii, and although drugs aren't hard to find, the Marines piss-test all the time and acid is the one thing you know that won't show up. This Motor T pogue, he could have been a narc from CID or NCIS or just some guy selling bogus shit, so you were nervous about meeting him in his quarters and doing the deal. You went to his room anyway. You didn't have a lot of options. He was a small guy, all tan skin and hair that he'd bleached with hydrogen peroxide from the PX. Star Trek was on TV and there was a surf board in the corner next to that ridiculously small fridge and furniture made by Lighthouse for the Blind everyone has in the barracks. Five bucks a hit, five hits in a cellophane wrapper from a pack of cigarettes. Little beige stamps with pictures of unicorns on them. You gave this surfer pogue mechanic twenty-five bucks and walked back to your car having just committed a felony on federal property that would get you ten to fifteen in Leavenworth if you were caught. You didn't think about it. You had other things on your mind. You drove your Mustang out past the flight line and back to your side of the base, the grunt side, where all the hard asses lived. Past KT, the radar station on top of that motherfucking hill they made you run up every morning. Past officer's wives in their convertibles and tennis skirts and debutante hair styles. Past new guys, Boots, walking to the E-club in their tight jeans and tank tops and fucked up high-and-tight haircuts that they still thought looked cool. Past captured Iraqi anti-aircraft guns parked in front of regimental headquarters to show that your unit had been there, done that.

You didn't keep any souvenirs from the war. Not tangible ones. Months and months of waiting in the heat like a coiled spring. Of being the bullet in the gun, waiting for your country to pull the trigger and let you loose. Finally it did, and you fired artillery and watched bombs fall on the enemy positions for a month before the long walk into Kuwait. The road was an apocalypse. Enemy bodies, sometimes whole, sometimes just pieces, littered the highway, their charred remains oozing from their vehicles like tar. Every third or fourth car you saw bones, or teeth, or part of a skull shining through the blackened flesh. Skeletal fingers still wrapped around a steering wheel where they'd clung while being burned alive. Did your shell do that? Were you the one who pulled the lanyard that sealed their fate? At the end of it, you'd sat down against a wall of sandbags and smoked cigarette after cigarette until your lungs burned. You thanked a god you don't believe in for getting you out alive and cursed him for letting the war happen in the first place. You were tired, you were one piece, and you told yourself that you wouldn't miss it. That being there didn't make you feel alive and powerful. You told yourself that, but you didn't believe it.

Three and a half years in The Suck, two deployments overseas and one war and you have had enough. Enough of guns and mind games and in six months you will get out and put it all behind you. The acid is part of that. Part of the effort to deprogram yourself from all the shit the Marines have put into your head. You've read that LSD changes the way you think about things for the rest of your life, and this sounds like a good thing. You read a survey somewhere about readjusting to civilian life after military service. Some people took six months to a year to fully adapt after separation. Those who saw combat took two to three years, this survey said. Sometimes longer. You know people who've never left it behind. Your father, who survived Vietnam but left part of himself there when he did, still talks about the Corps. You remember, as a child, asking him what the faded blue-black letters on his forearm meant. USMC in Old English script, just above a shrapnel scar.

Just like the letters on your arm.

You look up from hands that dug holes and held bodies and killed people, into the dark eyes of the girl at the bar. She looks like she knows, and you worry you've given everything away without saying a word. She's standing close enough for you to smell the coconut lotion on her skin. You wonder what her mouth feels like when she kisses. You wonder if you will have sex, and if you do, will she taste like coconut when you go down on her.

"What's your name?" You hope it's the first time you've asked her. Everything is in Technicolor and if you stare at the picture of the hula girl on the bar napkin she starts breathing.

The girl doesn't answer. She finishes her drink, puts down the glass and looks into your eyes. You think she's being romantic until she says, "You're in the middle of it, aren't you?"

"The middle of what?"

"Your trip," she says. "Your pupils are the size of dinner plates."

"My pupils?"

"I couldn't even guess what color your eyes are; everything's black."

"It's dark in here."

"It's not that dark," she says. "Let's go outside and get some air. I'm hot."

You follow her outside, past the giant Samoan bouncer at the front of the bar and out onto the street. Past pink neon words and the line to get in that stretches all the way down to the 7-Eleven. Cars honk as they drive by on Kalakaua Avenue and the girls in line wave back, blond hair and manicured fingernails strobe lighting under the streetlights. The girl leads you through the night, her ponytail blowing in the sea breeze like a barely contained thundercloud around her head. You want to hold her and have her hold you back so tight that you won't be able to breathe. You want to black out from her affection. You want to sit for hours and listen to her life story, her hopes, her dreams, anything; it doesn't matter. You just want to sit with a girl and remember what it feels like to be human again.

You have had your war. You have had your guns and your anger and your fear and you have had enough. Your time here is almost over. Soon you will leave and try to piece together what you used to be. What you used to dream about. You are leaving the Marines because you are afraid of what you've become. You're afraid of what happens next.

Tonight everything will change. Tonight everything will be different. Tonight this girl will take you home. Tonight you will begin peeling away the layers of military indoctrination and conditioning. Layers that will take years to fall away. Layers that you are afraid you will never be able to remove completely.

You must have been walking for a while now. The girl is talking and somehow you're at Lewers Street but you don't remember getting here. You can see other jarheads hanging around the entrance to Moose's, bullshitting with a local guy at the front door. A bouncer. You watch the four of them, a fire team, try to get hotel room numbers from a group of tourist chicks. You watch them get shot down and walk their sorry farmer-tanned asses to the ABC store in their boot camp running shoes, their names stamped on the side.

The girl stops. The light is red and she turns to fix you with her gaze.

"Do you ever read poetry?" she says.

"Not much," you say. "I usually stick to novels. I haven't read poetry since high school."

"You should."

"Really?"

"I love it," she says. "You read a poem just like a story, except in poetry, everything has a greater importance. Every word is a paragraph. Every syllable a sentence. Each comma, sound, letter, serves a purpose. Everything has meaning."

If you look hard enough, you think you can actually see the words coming out of her mouth as she says them. She starts to cross the street, but you have no idea what color the light is.

"Everything has meaning," you say, and follow her, one step behind, like a child.

On the sidewalk in front of the bank, a group of Hare Krishnas dance and pass out leaflets to tourists trapped in line at the ATM. You grab the girl's hand and start dancing with them, the acid in your brain making this seem like a perfectly sensible thing to do. This is dangerous, the streets are full of Marines and sailors, and any one of them could be CID or NCIS, but you don't care anymore. What are they going to do, kick you out? You keep chanting and swaying and the girl is laughing and holding your hand. You grab a flyer from one of the Krishnas and try to read it, but the words slip off of the page onto the sidewalk and swim towards the gutter like tadpoles. You stare at a picture of a man changing into a tiger into a fish into a beetle back into a man. You stare until your eyes burn and you actually see this person transforming in front of you and it's too much and you sit down on the pavement. You have a sudden realization that you hold the key to breaking this cycle right here in your hand. You think maybe you should find out more about this but you can't make out the phone number at the bottom of the paper. The girl touches your arm.

"You okay?"

You put the flyer into your pocket and look up at her.

She is hazy, ethereal, more spirit than flesh. "Yeah, let's go."

For the first time in years your mind is free of weapon nomenclatures, uniform regulations and the maximum effective range of your service rifle. You have been dancing and holding hands with this girl, a girl who probably doesn't care that you can hit nine out of ten head shots with your rifle from 500 meters in high wind. A girl who makes you feel human again.

The rest of the night becomes a blur. You and her, standing at the edge of the water, screaming at the breaking waves under a full moon. Trying to eat at Eggs 'n Things but not being able to get past the way the waffles keep moving when you try to stab them with your fork. Filling your mouth with food but never getting full. Watching her eat strawberries for ten minutes, ten hours, ten days, time no longer existing as the fruit stains her lips an illicit shade of red.

She takes you down to the beach and makes love to you on the sand. Everything becomes you and her and the wind, the stars, the sea. You reach back and release her ponytail, her hair cascading over your face like a dark curtain as she lowers her mouth onto yours, hips moving in rhythm with the waves crashing against the shore. Mouth on her neck, you taste salt and sweat and pull her closer to you with both hands until you explode and collapse on the sand. You sense, more than see, her stand up and kneel beside you. You feel like you should say something, but no words are coming forth. You keep trying, but she stops you with another kiss.

"Shhhhh," she says. "Shhhhh," and brushes your hair with her hands. You finally unclench your fists and stop trying to talk. Her voice is a whisper, fading into an echo as you close your eyes.

"All things are taken from us and become portions and parcels of the dreadful past."

The last thing you see are the stars getting larger, giant coronas spiraling outward, filling the black spaces of the sky in concentric circles of blinding luminescence.

The next morning I wake up on the beach. For a moment I think that the acid is still sticking to my brain but then I realize that the bright pink walls are normal; I'm outside of the Royal Hawaiian Hotel. I dust the sand off of my jeans and stumble towards the boulevard, hoping to find an early-morning ride back to the Windward side of the island. Back to Kaneohe Bay and the base. I remember the girl and her tattoo. Her smile. I close my eyes and her face becomes a bird, a fish, a butterfly, a girl again. I grab a taxi and make my way over the Pali Highway back to the Main Gate.

She Was Only a Bagel Seller's Daughter

She starts before the sun rises and sets out for the shop because the dough has to be made and the coffee started and the chairs set up and the customers always arrive before she's ready. The store is small but does good business and she can wear what she wants and the pay sucks but the management leaves her alone and these days, let's face it, you take what you can get if you want to survive.

She wants very much to survive.

By five o'clock the first commuters are standing in front of the doors with their travel mugs and their lousy tips and their phones full of audio books that will take them all the way to The City.

She thinks, *If I'm not careful, that's what will happen to me.*

Another hour, another hundred bagels, fifty with cream cheese, some with butter, some without.

The orders, they go on and on.

Do you have any non-dairy margarine? I'm vegan. Is this the only coffee you made today? It's too strong.

Are you going to play this music all morning? Do you have something else? I don't like it.

Her co-workers joke behind the counter. One is stoned, but still works very quickly which is something she can't comprehend; when she gets stoned she just wants to go to sleep. The other is four-months pregnant and knows she probably shouldn't be on her feet all day but the father-to-be is long gone and no one cares about your problems when the rent is due.

A screw fell out of her glasses this morning and she's trying to get by with a tiny safety pin to hold the arm in place and she hopes no one will notice and probably no one will but it's driving her crazy and making her a little self-conscious especially now when the guy she kind of likes comes in to buy his usual: cinnamon sugar bagel, toasted, butter, to go. She doesn't know his name, but he's nice to her and always tips, but only for her. Only if she's working the register when he orders. The safety pin feels like it's twenty-feet high as she takes his money and smiles and watches him go out the door to the rest of his day. His job. His life.

Someday she'll leave too.

By noon her feet are killing her but the lunch rush is in full swing and now sandwiches have to be made and the soda machine syrup is low and people are complaining about the slow service and the heat and traffic and their jobs and their spouses and the war and the president and that'll be $5.95, thank you very much have a nice day.

She knows that the secret to life is right there on the tip of her tongue but three different guys want to take her out tonight and she doesn't really like any of them but it's better than sitting at home staring at the walls and there's a movie out that she wants to see anyway.

She hates going to the movies by herself. Seeing the happy couples on their dates. Holding hands. Sharing popcorn. Sodas.

Kisses.

Midafternoon she sells a box of bagels to a Palestinian man who makes a comment about how ironic it is that he's buying food from a Jewish business and no one is worried about him blowing himself up. He leaves and she wonders what that must be like, to live in constant fear of someone walking into the store where you work and blowing up. It's a hard concept for her to grasp. Too distant from her world, like staring through a telescope the wrong way.

The afternoon, it goes mostly like this: clean the counter and wipe up a spilled chocolate milk that some kid knocked over before crying for another one that her dad bought her to shut her up and collect the newspapers from this morning left lying around in crumpled piles with photographs of the war dead splashed across page one like an ad for a new car and check her cell phone to see if anyone called (not that she's waiting for that guy from the other night to call back because that would be pathetic and no one did anyway) and back to the counter to wrap up the mayonnaise and the hot peppers and the cold slaw and the sprouts and take a break but don't smoke a cigarette because she's trying to quit but fuck it have one anyway and get mad because she had one and go back inside and try not to look at the clock because time crawls when your waiting to get off and it seems to her like she spends her whole life watching the clock and waiting but she doesn't know what for.

But it's right there.

On the tip of her tongue. Waiting.

Collateral Damage

My stepfather was outside watering the lawn with his shirt off and I could see his scars from the war. They spread out across his back like a map of some bizarre interstate highway. Shrapnel, he had told me once. Nothing more. I remembered begging for details as a boy, wanting to hear stories of glory and fighting for America, but he never indulged me.

"It was hot," he had said, "and a lot of my friends died. That's pretty much all you need to know."

He'd lost a lot of weight since I'd been home last. This giant, this mountain of freckles and a huge red moustache that loomed in my childhood, he was smaller than I was now. When he turned to look as I parked in the driveway I could see his ribs.

"Nice car," he said as I closed the door. My mother complained that he never used the oxygen tank like the doctor told him too, but his voice still sounded strong to me.

"It's a rental," I said. "They still don't pay me shit, you know how it is."

He nodded, held his hand out. I shook it like I always did: soul brother style like he had taught me years ago. The way he shook hands in the Marines. My fingers looked childlike wrapped around his.

He looked at the dirt on the front of my car. "You drove it up from Pendleton?"

I nodded.

"A long way to drive."

"Ten hours from the base to Sacramento." I looked at his skin, bright red from the hundred-degree July heat. "Eight if you drive like I do."

"Too long in a car for me. I'd fly."

"I needed the solitude."

He turned back to the lawn, watering spots that have been brown for years and always would be.

"You bring much luggage?"

"Just one bag, and a couple of suits."

He looked back over his shoulder at me. "Suits?"

"Yeah, well, my Blues."

He walked over to the faucet and turned the water off. He rolled the hose into a neat, one-foot circle and hung it alongside the house on a rack that was bracketed by two surgically trimmed manzanita bushes.

"Lawn needs trimming," he said. The grass couldn't have been more than an inch high.

I nodded. He turned to go inside and I followed. He stopped me.

"Get your things."

"They can wait, Red. I'll get them in a second."

He looked at me. "It's hot. Go get your bags and bring them inside before something melts."

I got my gear out of the trunk and brought it inside. He motioned for me to put it on the floor in the living room and I laid my suit bag over the back of a couch that was older than I was. My stepfather sat down in his recliner and breathed heavily.

"Need anything?" I said from the fridge.

"Get me a beer." His voice betrayed the effort that watering the lawn had taken.

"Are you sure that's okay with, you know…?"

"No, but it doesn't really matter now, does it?"

I took two bottles out of the fridge and gave him one. I watched hands that I'd seen break boards and crush cans and leave bruises strain to open the twist off bottle cap. His chest was sunken, and I wanted to ask him to put a shirt on but I just opened my own beer and took a long drink instead.

"Well," he said, "someone finally gave you a decent haircut, didn't they?"

"It's been this way for a few years now."

"Yeah, I guess it has."

I could hear the grandfather clock ticking in the hallway.

"Where's Mom?"

"Store," he said. "She's getting stuff for dinner. You staying?"

"Yeah, sure." I said. "I don't really have anything planned tonight."

He took a long pull from his beer. "You going to go see your dad while you're out here?"

I looked around. The only thing that had changed since I'd left was a new, giant-screen television dominating one corner of the living room. My mother had written me saying that my stepfather watched golf on it all day. She didn't bother him about it because he was too weak to play anymore. I knew she hated the television, that they couldn't really afford it, but how could she tell him no?

"Yeah," I said. "I'll probably make it up to the mountains to see him at least once this week I guess."

He turned the television on but muted the sound. In his hands the remote looked like a deck of cards. There was a documentary on. Black and white soldiers ran across black and white battlefields. My stepfather snorted and drank his beer.

"Well," he said. "You going to show me or not?"

"Show you what?"

"You know you want to show me, that's why you brought the damn thing here, isn't it?" He pointed at my suit bag with his beer bottle.

"I just got here," I said. "Mom will want to see it too. I can wait."

"One thing I've learned these past few months," he said, "is there's no point in waiting, if you know what I mean." He smiled, but there was something in his eyes I'd never seen before: resignation. Not defeat—he would never stop fighting—but an acceptance that his condition was not simply going to go away on its own.

I walked over to my bag, unzipped it, and pulled back the flap. Silver and brass shined back at me from a dark blue field. I carefully removed my uniform and laid it on the couch where he could see it.

"Yep," he said. "Looks just like I remember it."

He stood up, looked closely at my ribbons. Years of my life condensed into small bits of colored cloth and tiny stars. Commemorations of brutal acts in faraway places that someone thought were worth it. I could feel heat rising in my face. It was difficult to breathe properly. He bent down to look closer and I could see the puckered scar on his back, a bullet wound from a lifetime ago.

"You really earned these?" he said. "They didn't just give them to you for long-distance marching, or being a good runner, or some chickenshit like that, right?" He looked up at me, back down at the uniform, busting my balls with his sarcasm.

"You know what those are," I said. "You aren't that old. You still remember what some of those mean." My voice sounded funny. I hoped I was the only one who noticed.

"Yeah," he said, sitting back down in his chair. "I remember what some of those mean." He took a drink from his beer. "I even remember what it takes to get them."

"You been watching it on TV?" I said.

"What, the war?"

I nodded.

"No," he said. "I've seen the real thing, I don't need to see it on the news twenty-four hours a day told by people who don't know what the business end of a rifle looks like."

I thought about the guys in my platoon who had learned the hard way what an enemy rifle could do to a human being. Or a land mine. Or a bomb. I thought about the letters I'd written to their families, the dog tags I'd collected. I remembered the eighteen-year-old PFC who died in my arms waiting for the medevac to arrive, his blood soaking into the sand beneath us. I wondered how many letters my stepfather had written in his war. How many faces he still saw at night. I finished my beer and put the empty bottle in the garbage. Red was still staring at the ribbons on my uniform.

"No purple heart," he said.

"Someone once told me that those were for people who didn't know when to duck."

"I guess my advice worked." He turned to face me, iron-gray stubble lined his cheeks. Until that day, I had never seen him anything but clean-shaven.

"I guess so."

I thought about close calls: ambushes, vehicle accidents, impossible heat and the constant, horrifying threat of IEDs that still had me obsessively checking the road all the way up from Southern California. I remembered boredom, touch football games in the desert, and hearing who'd won the Super Bowl days after it was over.

I remembered killing my first human being.

"Hey." My stepfather brought me back from my reverie. "Whatever anyone says, you done good, kid."

"You don't know what I did."

"I know you're here," he said. "I know you're alive and I sure as shit know better than you do that's all that matters." He took another pull from his beer and went on. "So later on, when you feel bad about what happened over there, you just remember that at least you're alive to feel it."

His voice sunk into my bones, a rich, strong baritone, and for a moment there was no sickness, no oxygen tank. No six months to live. For a moment he was the man who'd taught a boy how to bait a hook, how to stand up to a bully and fight back. The man who'd stood in front of a bedroom wall covered with neatly framed medals and citations and told me that he thought I was crazy for joining the Marines. The man who'd driven me to the recruiting station the day I'd shipped out, shook my hand and told me something my real father never had: that he was proud of me.

Red raised his bottle. "Welcome home, kid," he said, and finished off the last of his beer.

Later that year, after my stepfather died, I came home again to take care of the arrangements because my mother wasn't able. I collected his things from hospice. I wrote his obituary, the eulogy, and arranged for a Marine honor guard at his funeral. I stood next to my mother in my dress blues when the sergeant handed her the flag. She had never allowed herself to cry during Red's illness, told herself that she wouldn't during the ceremony, but when the honor guard leaned over and made the presentation "On behalf of a grateful nation. . ." she wasn't able to hold back anymore.

But this would all come in the future. Back then, in my parents' house, I didn't know any of that. At that moment, Red and I sat there, watching another war on television. A war where the good guys won, the bad guys lost, and all of the heroes went home alive and in one piece.

We sat there together, waiting for my mother to come home, two Marines from two different wars, each with their own scars.

ACKNOWLEDGMENTS

It's a cliché that writing is done alone in a room, but I am fortunate enough to have had the help and encouragement of many people during the crafting of these stories. Huge thanks to my wife, Kendra, for her constant encouragement and support in all areas of my life. To Jeff Hess, who, since graduate school, has taken time from his own writing to help me with mine. To Tracy Crow for keeping hope alive when I thought this project was at an end. To the editors and publishers of the journals and anthologies where many of these stories first appeared, thank you for giving me a chance. Lastly, to Marines everywhere, but especially those I served with. I still owe all of you a beer.

Photo courtesy of the author

ABOUT THE AUTHOR

Kevin C. Jones' work has been featured in a variety of literary journals and anthologies, including the *New York Times*, and *Red, White, & True: Stories from Veterans & Families, WWII to Present*. A former Marine, he holds an MFA from Queens University of Charlotte and a PhD from the University of Florida. Kevin lives and works in Florida's Tampa Bay area.

Thank you for supporting the creative works of veterans and military family members by purchasing this book. If you enjoyed your reading experience, we're certain you'll enjoy these other great reads.

SALMON IN THE SEINE
by Norris Comer

One moment 18-year-old Norris Comer is throwing his high school graduation cap in the air and setting off for Alaska to earn money, and the next he's comforting a wounded commercial fisherman who's desperate for the mercy of a rescue helicopter. From landlubber to deckhand, Comer's harrowing adventures at sea and during a solo search in the Denali backcountry for wolves provide a transformative bridge from adolescence to adulthood.

CRY OF THE HEART
by RLynn Johnson

After law school, a group of women calling themselves the Alphas embark on diverse legal careers—Pauline joins the Army as a Judge Advocate. For twenty years, the Alphas gather for annual weekend retreats where the shenanigans and truth-telling will test and transform the bonds of sisterhood.

BEYOND THEIR LIMITS OF LONGING
by Jennifer Orth-Veillon

The first collection of poetry, fiction, and nonfiction to reveal the important, yet often overlooked, influence of World War One on contemporary writers and scholars—many of them post-9ll veterans. Among the contributors are Pulitzer Prize-winning and National Book Award-winning authors.

SUB WIFE
by Samantha Otto Brown

A Navy wife's account of life within the super-secret sector of the submarine community, and of the support among spouses who often wait and worry through long stretches of silence from loved ones who are deeply submerged.

www.ingramcontent.com/pod-product-compliance
Lightning Source LLC
Chambersburg PA
CBHW021736190726
48288CB00009B/3075